For two of the great ladies

In my life.

Mom for never stop believing in me.

The Sophie for giving me something to believe.

All Good Things

by John G. Walker

This is a work of fiction. Any resemblances to any actions, places, or persons living or dead is purely coincidental. That includes restaurants, hospitals, family members, and pretty much anything between "Chapter" and "support". In other words, folks, don't take this seriously. It's a story, not real life.

Acknowledgements/Foreword

Hello again, good people. This was not an easy one to write, as you'll see in the following pages. Don't get me wrong; I knew I could write it. My cheerleading section is a hell of a lot bigger than I deserve. What I mean is: this book changes everything.

I've written four and a half books in this series, and this one makes five and a half. I know how this story goes, I know where it goes, and I know how it ends. It's not all sunshine and lollipops, folks, and I guess this hammers that point home pretty succinctly.

Where am I going with this? Simple: I just want you all to know that there is a plan, and there is a point to all of this. It's kind of like the way life is. Good things happen to bad people, and bad things happen to good people. Sometimes, you can strike that and reverse it, and everything evens out in the end.

I got asked a lot about the plan, like it's something from the Cylons from Battlestar Galactica. I will admit, it's pretty grandiose. There's a lot to the whole thing, and there will be a couple of offshoots from it, mostly stories from other characters' points of view. Only two people know the endgame, and I won't tell you who they are. Suffice it to say, it's going to be one hell of a ride. Now, to recognize those to thank and/or blame for making these words and ideas possible.

My mom, who is about ten times more badass than Tom's mom.

My niece, who keeps me trying to be the cool uncle she deserves.

My grandmother, who would totally start the RVF Foundation.

My sister and brother-in-law for answering legal questions for me, and encouraging me.

My editor, Erika Pryor, who made me focus, and got everything stapled together without a single visible seam.

My cover artist, Starla Huchton, for yet another incredible work of art, which pushes me to write a book worthy of being wrapped in it.

Those fantastic and fabulous people of the RoTaNoWriMo group. Your comments and ideas made this possible.

And of course, as always, to my faithful readers. You who enjoy hopping into this parallel world I've spun, you are all awesome party people. These words are because of you.

Now, my friends and neighbors, it's time to strap in and hang on. This is going to be a very bumpy ride. As always, thank you for your support. It means more than you all will know.

-jgw

Chapter One

I am entirely too nice.

I let people get away with entirely too much. I'm a sucker for my niece and nephew, as their parents would attest. I help my landlord find out what his flavor-of-the-month girlfriend was doing before she became the flavor. I also let potential clients ramble on until they stop to catch a breath before telling them whether I will or won't take their case.

As an example, take the broad-shouldered older man who has been pacing back and forth for twenty minutes, explaining in way too much excruciating detail just why I should take his case. Not only that, he hinted in as breathless as one could get, when they could shatter a mountain with their voice, that it was a matter of global, nay (his phrasing), universal importance that I work for him. The long strides across the threadbare carpet of my office were quite impressive, as was the glorious streaming ponytail of silver behind him. The full beard was neatly trimmed, groomed to the perfection that made strong men weak and good girls knees buckle. His suit was impeccably tailored, completely form-fitted to his powerful frame, his shoes shined to a mirror finish. He had the air of someone use to always getting his way, as if his word was universal law.

That made sense of course, you know, since he was a god.

Sitting with my feet up on my desk, I had listened patiently to the diatribe, alternating my gaze between him and the clock on the wall which read very nearly five o'clock. As I didn't have a case, I kept banker's hours the last several months since coming back from New Orleans. I could still feel the simmering anger in my chest from the way I had been suckered into doing dirty work for deities who really did not give one iota of a damn for my well-being. Case in point, the one storming back and forth, to and fro, complaining that I wasn't fulfilling my duties.

When the god had finished his rant, I raised my eyebrows and said, "Are you done?" See? I was nice enough to wait for him to stop talking.

"I most certainly am not!" Thunder rolled from his voice and lightning danced in his eyes.

I nodded my head. "Yeah, you are." Before he could speak again, I held up a silencing hand. For a wonder, it worked. "Who are you?"

The deity swelled to his rather imposing six-and-a-half foot height and puffed up his barrel chest. "You know exactly who I am!"

A thin smile crossed my lips. "Humor me."

Mighty hands clenched and I heard the sizzle of electricity in the place of cracking knuckles. "I am Zeus, Master of Olympus, father of the gods, lord of thunder and lightning! I who have fathered heroes and gods still spoken of in awe and wonder am here to command your service to me, as I have my sons Perseus and Heracles before!"

Command me. Oh yeah, that's going to get in my good graces. Besides, I had heard such a résumé before; it was nothing new. "And who am I?" I yawned.

"You are Thomas Statford, the Keeper of the Conclave!" The words boomed in the small office, rattling the windows and spilling papers to the ground. "You are the chosen representative between the gods and mortals, the one who was decreed to be the one who assists the divine and the mundane as needed!"

Zeus made being the Keeper sound so much more awesome than it actually was. I had been drafted to be the one who "assisted" all the gods of common and not-so-common myth in whatever issues they might have with mortals, or as was usually the case, save mortals from getting their idiot asses killed or worse by getting involved with the gods. In the years I have had the mantle of the Keeper, I had been shot, stabbed, beaten, tortured, exposed to a demon, punched by said demon, stabbed again, seared, and otherwise damaged almost beyond belief but never beyond recovery. Whether that was a sign of my resilience or just my being too stupid to give up was a matter of some debate.

I tried to explain it once to my friend Jim MacPherson, a cop I had known for years and called one of my greatest friends. The gods exist. All of them that have ever been thought of, pondered or worshipped were around, and they all had roughly the same amount of power, which was a pure nuclear crapload, and the maturity level of a three-year-old child. When they realized that their temper tantrums that destroyed galaxies and trillions of beings were starting to get out of hand, the gods decided to calm down and create a sort of mutual non-aggression pact they called the Conclave. This was mainly to keep the universe going in a non-blown-up direction, but also to make sure no one group got more power than the other. Pantheons could get so pissy that way.

To make certain no one god could get a leg up over any other, the powers that be chose a mortal to be their impartial mediator, and for nigh upon six thousand years or so, give or take, the Keeper had held the line between gods and mortals. In those centuries, one Keeper after another had been chosen, seemingly at random, all in the attempt to make sure the gods didn't have too much fun, or mortals didn't end up lunch, broodmares, playthings or worse. That is pretty damned near a full-time job.

By and large, though, it wasn't a bad gig, depending on who you asked. If the gods were asked, they would have said I was a whiny toad who had no idea how lucky I was to have been afforded such a great and awesome responsibility. If the average mortal were asked, they likely would have thought it exciting and amazing and wonderful, just like they saw in the movies.

If I was asked, the response would be so laden with profanity, Joe Pesci would tell me to tone it down. I had reason to hate the job, and of anyone, the father of the Greek gods should know exactly why I was about to turn him down.

"I've been very patient with you," I said, bringing my feet to the floor. "I've let you have your say, Zeus. I've entertained your request, pondered it, and gave it due consideration." His face seemed to light up in anticipation of my answer. "In fact, I even reconsidered it while you did the booming voice thing that scares the rubes. Rather nice touch, by the way." I put my hands flat on my desk and looked up at the god of lightning and thunder and said in my most calm voice, "The answer is this: Get the fuck out of my office."

It was like watching a kid at Christmas open up a box the size of a bicycle and see that it was full of ugly sweaters. His disgustingly perfect, angular face fell like the bolts holding it together had been loosened and tossed aside, his jaw dropped, and a strangled cry escaped his throat. He whispered, almost inaudibly, "What did you say?"

"I said get out. Leave. Be gone from my sight, if that gets your formal-speaking motor running!" My voice climbed on each word, venom lacing my voice. I pulled myself to my nearly six feet and shouted into his face, "You people have no fucking shame whatsoever! I nearly lost my entire family to a two-bit witch doctor down in New Orleans because you pricks fucking sent me there!" Spittle flew from my lips, and I was sure my normally dark-brown eyes were black as pitch. "I would have been fine if someone had asked me beforehand, so I knew I had to do something! But no! You bastards thought it would be cute to con me into doing a job for you. Why? Tell me why?"

"It was necessary to---" Zeus began, but I cut him off with my own words.

"To teach the stupid mortal Keeper who was in charge!" I was furious, running my hands through my brown hair. "You come in here, telling me what I had to do, what I must do, what you command me to do! Apparently Hermes didn't get you the message, Beard Boy: I fucking quit. I quit months ago. There is no more Keeper, there is no more Tom Statford working for the high-and-mighty Conclave, there is no more bullshit of being forced to dance like a fucking puppet on a string for a bunch of over-powered and immature children. Do you understand?" He could have told me I was going to win the lottery and find the cure for cancer, and I still would have cut him off. Some gods or their representatives may forgive and forget. Some may think it's a good thing to turn the other cheek. That is not, nor will it ever be, my way.

"You are not to speak to me this way!" Zeus roared at me, trying to push me back with the force of his voice. "This is outrageous!"

"This is life, you silly son of a bitch. This is the consequence of suckering me into working for you. This is part of what happens when you threaten the people I love." I pointed my finger at the door, snarling. "Don't let it hit you in the ass on the way out."

Zeus put his fists on the top of my desk, hunching over to try to intimidate me. "You are choosing very poorly, Keeper." I could see the muscles rippling under the suit; either he was going to fight or he was going to walk. The way I felt, I was okay with either.

"Go ahead, motherfucker." I balled up my fists and let a smile come over me. "Take your best shot."

The father of Olympus seemed to bite back a reply, and I knew there was nothing he could really do about it. None of the gods could hurt me directly, which was part of the benefits package of being the Keeper. Oh, they could try making my life miserable, even more than they had already, they could leave me twisting in the wind at an inopportune time, but that would leave room for the other gods of the Conclave to make nice and possibly increase their power and standing. It was kind of like a high school social ladder, in a roundabout sort of way.

I hated high school.

The door to my office slammed in thunderous rage as Zeus left; I could see sparks flying off the ends of his hair and beard. He had been vehement that I help him find one of his trinkets he had lost, likely on the nightstand of some woman he had seduced an indeterminate time before. Zeus was a randy old bugger, though imperious when he believed he wasn't getting what he wanted.

I couldn't even muster the desire to give a damn what he wanted or how he felt. I had wanted a nice little vacation where people weren't trying to kill me and weren't dropping dead around me.

A voice, calm and studied, spoke from behind me. "You certainly have a way with people." The words were bemused and tinged with sadness.

"That wasn't people, Larry. That was an asshole god who wanted me to find his mystic doodad so his bitch-queen wife wouldn't get on his case. Again."

"While not inaccurate, that is not the best way to characterize them. It will win you no friends."

I turned and faced my friend and, though he would sputter in derision at the description, sidekick. Larrisimus, or Larry as I called him, was timeless as usual. He was leaning against the wall, his arms crossed as he looked at me in both exasperation and bemusement. His blonde hair that brushed his shoulders was a bit longer than I had last seen it; perhaps he was trying something new. A smooth brow above piercing blue eyes and thin lips rounded out his features. He was dressed in a suit similar to Zeus's, though Larry's was a royal purple and the shoes were suede in the same shade. Larry was a six thousand year old spirit, and had been a Keeper's constant companion from one to the next. While I hadn't been sure how my resignation would affect things between us when I had done it, there seemed to be no change in the status quo. I wasn't quite sure how to take that, but I wasn't about to look a gift horse in the mouth.

"I didn't know I was supposed to be making friends, Larry." I pushed away from my desk and began tidying up a bit. The ring on my finger clinked on the handle of a coffee cup reminding me of what had been instrumental in my decision to tell the Conclave to piss off. The small living area off my office had been turned into more of a storage place since I had moved in with my wife Susana. As I pushed open the door, I said over my shoulder, "Didn't they hear that I had told them in no uncertain terms that I was done with their bullshit?"

Larry raised an eyebrow and sighed. "You must understand, Thomas, never in history has a Keeper given up the mantle. It is absolutely unheard of, and there has been much consternation over your decision. Six times you have been approached by the Conclave, and six times you have refused them." The spirit uncrossed his arms and walked toward me, making no sound unlike the deity that had been unceremoniously thrown out on his ass. "No one is quite sure what to think about it, or you."

I set the cup in the sink and came back into the office; I could wash it later. "That is not my problem, Larry. Not anymore," I said, wiping my hands on a towel.

"I can only tell you what I know, Thomas." Larry held up his hands in a placating gesture. "I have no idea what they might or might not do. The Conclave could simply wait until you expire naturally and a new Keeper would be chosen."

"So you mean until the day I die, I'm going to have these chuckleheads knocking at my door asking me to fix their problems?"

"They could cease after a period of time," Larry said hopefully. "It is possible."

"What's the other option?'

Larry hesitated, then continued at a glare from me. "They could force you to get involved."

"They did that already." I looked at Larry and clenched my fists.

"And they could do it again, Thomas. This time more forcefully." Larry looked nervously at me, then into my eyes. He stepped back with a gasp under my gaze.

I snarled as I advanced on the spirit. "They can try, and I will make the heavens fall." I felt a sharp pain in my left palm. Larry broke the gaze first and looked down. I followed his eyes to my clenched fist. Blood dripped from underneath my fingers where the nails had bitten into the flesh of my palm.

That pain brought me back to what passed for reality. With an effort, I unlocked my fingers and saw the trio of crimson crescents I had made. Flexing my hand and digits to get the feeling back, I hissed at the stings of pain. It hurt, but what hurt more was how badly the Conclave's betrayal had affected me. Of course they would never call it that; as far as they were concerned, I was merely the hired help. The gods looked on all mortals as disposable, and I was apparently more disposable than most. That was not the best way to get in my good graces, and it sure as hell would not get me to take back the mantle of the Keeper.

I went to my desk to grab a tissue. No need for my wife to think I had gotten hurt for any reason, as she might have beat the hell out of me for it. As I dabbed at the wounds, I winced, both at the pain and at my own anger. I realized the gods would not likely try anything as extreme as going after my family. That would be beyond the pale and even they wouldn't stoop so low. Manipulation was their usual stock in trade those days; direct action was not their style. The days of the burning bush and the talking lightning bolts were long over.

"I'm going home, Larry." The blood had stopped flowing as freely since I had packed the wounds with the flimsy tissue, but the anger was still fresh. "I'm going to go home and relax and have dinner with Susana. After that, I don't know, but I will not have any weirdness going on. Not anymore."

"One day, you may wake up and not have that choice, Thomas." Damn his cultured tones. He had to sound so reasonable.

And of course, he just had to be right.

Chapter Two

I was still in a high state of pissed when I pulled my coat on. Though Larry was likely right, it didn't mean I had to like it. I shut off my computer and locked up my laptop out of habit. Though my usual clientele could miracle any information they wanted out of my electronics, I sometimes dealt with mortal scum of the earth as well.

"Thomas, this is not the best way to handle things." Larry walked after me, his footfalls silent while mine thundered on the floor. "Much as I am loathe to agree with the Conclave, and as much as I agree and understand your anger, outright refusing the requests of the Conclave is utter lunacy. The Conclave will find a way to get you involved again. You truly have no choice."

I put my keys in my pants pocket, trying not to jab my thigh with them. "Don't give me that shit, Larry. Six months, six gods, and each one has been kicked to the curb. I'm making my choice for the right reasons, and it's the right choice. I refuse to be their bitch."

Larry sighed as I put my phone in my coat pocket. "That is not what you were or are. You are an integral part of the nature of this world, Thomas. You are upsetting the balance of the universe by fighting the Conclave. It is unwise and very likely unhealthy to make this choice."

"Screw the universe. Whatever god is responsible for humanity gave us free will, and the means to act on it," I spat back. "I'm acting on that free will and telling the whole thing to just kiss my ass. There is absolutely no way I'm going back. I have had enough." I pulled my coat closed and buttoned it against the elements. It was one of those long black leather coats that looked great and actually kept me warm. Susana had given it to me on my birthday and insisted I wear it, saying I looked like one of those old Western gunslingers.

Admittedly, I had to wonder, if only in a morbidly curious way, why the Conclave didn't just accept my resignation and find someone else to torture. Usually when someone decides to quit a job, their employers shrug and find some other poor schlub to hire. Since July, once a month, a different god had come into my office, trying to get help from me for some trivial matter that they believed was of cosmic importance. Zeus, for example, was missing one of his cufflinks. Like I said, a trivial matter, unless you're married to a goddess who was known to be a cosmic-level witch about your philandering, plus you're too much a horndog to knock it the hell off and just nail your goddess of a wife instead of every piece of tail that your eye happens to catch. That he likely dropped it in some supermodel's hotel room either pre- or post-coitus wasn't the issue.

The problem was which supermodel. The dude got around.

A deep breath helped clear my mind a bit. All of that was behind me, and I was a regular private detective for regular people, not deities who could bend reality with their nose hairs. I knew why the gods had me do the quick "find this, get that" jobs. It was simply that they felt such tasks were beneath them, and since I was a mortal, they could have me handle menial tasks. After all, why waste infinite power and influence on something mundane when there's a mortal who can do your bidding? It was thoughts and ideas like that which made my decision that much easier to make.

I pulled the door open to the cold winter day, the wind briskly spraying a spattering of snow over the parking lot. Winters were always my least favorite season in Virginia, as the weather never could figure out if it was supposed to be bright and cold, bright and pleasant, cloudy and cold, or any combination that would cause everyone to get the flu at least twice. That day, it was snow, and not the kind of snow that allowed for snowmen and snow forts with snowball fights. It was bitterly cold and the white flakes were sharp crystals flying horizontally, making my face feel like it was under attack by a thousand paper cuts. Fortunately, I had had presence of mind enough to park close to my office door.

Since Mr. Martoukas, the incessant double-parker who ran the antique store two doors down from me, had retired over the summer, the parking lot felt very empty. I knew Mr. Martoukas's son Brian took the bus to get to the shop, so there was only my car, the Black Beauty. She was old, a 1998 Chevy Tracker two-door, but I kept her because she was dependable and was almost like family. I knew it was a silly way to feel about a car, but she was paid for and she started every time.

She was also not where I parked her.

I looked across the lot and saw the Beauty. She was at the far end of the lot, half-covered in snow and ice. The contrast of the white on the black paint was jarring, though not as jarring as seeing my car parked in a place I knew I hadn't parked. That got the alarms in my head ringing. My hand went under my coat to my shoulder rig, where my Beretta pistol was holstered. The checkerboard grips were a comfort on my palm, though I didn't pull the weapon out right then. I didn't discount the possibility I could have parked in a different place that afternoon after lunch. Forgetfulness happened to most people, even me.

I checked where I had originally parked and narrowed my eyes. Something about the tracks caught my eye, so I hunkered down to look at them, unmindful of the cold and how the wind made the tails of the coat flutter. The tracks seemed to be fresh, and there was still a bit of blacktop visible where the tires had been. I had heard the first bits of snow starting two hours prior, so even though it hadn't reached blizzard conditions, there would be no parking lot untouched by snow. The tracks also seemed to show the Beauty backing up and driving toward where she sat. That made me nervous. I stood up and began to walk slowly to the Beauty, trying to look in all directions to see if anyone was watching.

That was when my car and my whole godsdamned world erupted into a fireball. A really big frigging fireball. The Beauty erupted in a gout of flame, the pillar reaching at least twice as tall as I was. My car rode that flame, bending in half from the heat and pressure. The axles shattered from the force of the explosion, the brand new snow tires shredding like so much rubber confetti. My arms flew up in front of my face automatically in the first few fractions of a second, and I felt small pokes against my arms and chest. In the time I had to think, I realized those were the remains of my tires, the air inside them superheated to cause them to explode. The sounds of the tires bursting were lost in the main explosion, a fiery cataclysm just a few scant yards away.

In that way that high stress situations do, time slowed down enough for me to catch everything. The flash of the explosion hit me first, dazzling my eyes. The shockwave struck me like a runaway train, throwing me about a dozen feet through the air. As I flew like Superman on a tequila bender, my mind raced. Was I okay? Did any shrapnel hit me? Was anyone else hurt?

At the apex of my "flight", the worst question hit me: Was any of my family being targeted as well?

I tried to brace myself for striking the ground, which came up to meet me much too quickly. Twisting in mid-air may work in the movies, but not so much for me as the unforgiving blacktop rushed for me and I couldn't get my arms to do more than cover my head. The snow wasn't much of a cushion, but my coat helped soften the hit a little. Not much, but a little.

I rolled as I landed in a heap, coming to a breathless rest on my back. White flakes began covering my face as I tried to get my wind back. My lungs hurt and it felt like they would never get full again. I felt my heart beating like a jackhammer and adrenaline, a bit late to the party, coursing through my blood. It left me as suddenly as it came, making the world go gray.

The hollow sound of darkness, blood and pain. All around me, nothing but blood and pain.

And death. I can't forget that. I can never forget that. Death had been my constant companion and we hadn't even officially met. There was a dripping coming from somewhere nearby, so close, invisible and maddening with the constant sound, like a hollowed thump that never stops, never quits, no matter what is done to the muscle that creates it.

A heart like mine.

I watched in horror as it happened, my eyes not able to close, no longer from the thugs who had held me down and kept my head straight with strong hands, keeping my eyelids open with their fingers. My throat was raw, from crying, from screaming, I didn't know or care. Sobs still wracked my body with harsh pain and frequency. My arms, bare after my coat and shirt were ripped from my chest, were covered in a mixture of bruises, scrapes and blood, little of it my own. I strained against the bonds around my wrists, feeling the leather tighten around them, hearing the clinking of the chains as I hitched in another breath to scream.

My eyes flew open and I pulled breath into my lungs, out of the black, out of the pain. I felt t my heart race through my chest. The frost in my lungs along with the stench of burning metal made each breath increasingly difficult.

When I woke up, I didn't know how badly I was hurt, if at all, but I pushed the idea away. Endorphins were something I was used to having my body produce, and they were likely doing their job of being painkillers. I couldn't hear anything, which didn't surprise me either. I was rather calm, all things considered. That was likely the endorphins, too.

So I laid there in the snow, not wanting to move quite yet. Being present on the outskirts of an explosion was a novel experience for me, and I wasn't quite sure how to react. I could smell the burning metal and plastic of the Beauty's funeral pyre, acrid and bitter on the wind. My eyelids opened and immediately shut, the blast of cold wind nearly freezing my watering eyes solid. I slowly started wiggling fingers and toes, turning my head left and right, letting all my senses report in. My ears still weren't working, as I didn't hear the gasp of pain as I lifted my head up to make sure I still had all my parts. I marveled at the skidmarks through the snow my body made, and was amazed I wasn't chunky salsa.

In the calmness I felt the anger start to build, but I tamped it back down. Anger would get me nowhere, or worse, it would get me killed. Admittedly it was a struggle to not jump up and scream at the world, but I kept my cool, counting slowly down from one hundred.

I would use the anger as I would any other emotion: as a goad to focus.

This would not go well. Someone had blown up my car to send me a message.

They had my complete attention.

Chapter Three

The ringing in my ears had mostly gone away by the time the cops showed up. That's one of the big things nobody ever sees in movies: the aftermath of an explosion. Usually there's a cut with the hero to another scene and he can hear a mouse fart in church. The high-pitched tone in my ears told me that while I could still hear, there was a certain frequency that I would never hear again. That just made me angrier.

I was sitting on the back bumper of the ambulance that had been dispatched. There were two hospitals nearby and there were always ambulances driving around. I made some small talk with one of the paramedics as I observed Hampton's finest walking around the still smoldering ruins of the Black Beauty, still too hot to get near. I was still in shock, more mental than physical by then. Someone had blown up my car, and to my knowledge, I hadn't pissed anyone off recently that used car bombs.

Waving off the EMT, I stood up slowly. I still felt like shit, but at least I could feel. That's another thing they don't show in the movies. When you get hit by a shockwave, it stays with you for a long time. Your equilibrium is off, you end up compensating for one reason or another by making exaggerated movements or by being comically careful. I likely looked like an invalid as I shuffled, and the resulting self-deprecating chuckle hurt my chest. The pain helped focus me.

The snow still fell, and the cold burned across my face. I winced as I made my way to one of the cops on the scene, who had cordoned off everything in a fifty foot radius, with my car at the center. She was scribbling in a notebook while I approached, but stopped as she heard my staggering. Granted, I hadn't been trying to sneak up on her, but hearing someone approach on snow when moving somewhat slowly meant either my hearing was completely screwed, or she was very much on edge. Looking at the twisted metal and plastic remains of the Black Beauty, I was thinking it was likely the latter.

"You okay, Statford?" Rika Elder's greeting was perfunctory, one I'd more expect if I had skinned my knee or gotten stung by a bee. Shorter than me by half a foot but deceptively strong, Rika went back to scribbling. She had been with the Special Cases Unit for six months, a transfer from Tennessee. A decorated officer, we had worked together once when she had first gotten on the force years ago in Memphis. I hadn't talked to her much over the years, as she had stayed in Tennessee while I had returned to my old stamping grounds of Virginia. She was tough and brooked no bullshit, which made me respect her all the more. Rika was dressed in complete contrast to the weather, her black clothing and dark skin clashing with the white of the precipitation. She had her hair pulled back tightly and looked back over the rims of her glasses at me. "Didn't rattle your cage too hard, I hope."

I chuckled and shook my head, sending a wave of dizziness through me. "Take more than that to keep me down for the count." I put my hand out on the hood of a nearby police cruiser to steady myself. "Any ideas?"

"Bomb Squad is looking into it, so we might not know for a while." Rika studiously kept her eyes on the guttering flames. "This was pretty serious."

"Looks that way," I allowed.

"You piss someone off?" She paused, then added, "Again?"

That brought a smile. "I've been asking myself that, and as far as I know, this is the most pedestrian way someone would show me their displeasure with my continued existence."

"So that's a no." Rika shrugged and wrote a bit more. After a moment, she said, "You know she knows, right?"

"Yeah." This, like so much else that evening, would not go well.

"Only reason she's not here yet is she was up in Williamsburg." Rika smiled. "She's gonna be pissed."

"Probably."

Glancing sidelong at me, Rika said, "You want me to have the boys zap her once or twice to calm her down?"

I laughed then, which turned into coughing. "No, please don't. That will just make her angrier."

A siren approached from Rip Rap Road, and I knew who it was. With the ambulance, fire department and various cops already present, there could be only one person driving like a lunatic to the scene of an explosion. I heard the screeching of brakes and the sound of a pissed-off Mexican woman screaming a mixture of English and Spanish cuss words at anyone who got in her way. One of the uniformed officers working the barriers made the dumbest mistake of his life and career.

He tried to stop her.

Susana Magdalena Statford came to a skidding halt. While not a towering specimen of womanhood at under five and a half feet tall, her eyes blazed with the force of a squadron of helicopters while Wagner's Flight of the Valkyries played at ear-splitting volume. She seemed to be steaming in the cold wind, staring up into the eyes of the rookie who probably didn't know any better, but was about to find just how bad his life was going to get. Susana was wiry, her form hidden under jeans and a thick coat, but she might as well have been built like Hercules for the way she put her fists on her hips.

"Aw, shit," I muttered. She was going to kill him if he didn't move, and I had to go save the kid. I started moving at a slow limp.

"Out of the way, rookie," she growled. My hearing was coming back; I heard her just fine. I especially heard the threat of immediate dismemberment if the kid held her up any more than he already had.

"Sorry, ma'am, orders say no one's allowed back there." I had to give him credit. He had not balked or wavered, which most people do when dealing with Susana. My wife was one of the most decorated officers on the force, having been instrumental in taking down a serial killer, a corrupt televangelist, and a Triad crime boss. She had faced off against some of the worst and strangest things this world had to offer and had not blinked. Tough as steel, and unstoppable if she didn't get her way.

"Orders from who, *pinche*?" Susana's eyes narrowed dangerously.

"From the OIC," the kid said. "I mean, the officer in charge. Civilians and press are to stay back in case there's further problems. Sorry, ma'am." The kid then crossed his arms and looked down at Susana, whose mouth had dropped open in shock.

It was about then I realized that the kid just didn't know who she was. Not only that, but he thought that some random civilian was going to just walk into a crime scene and start pushing people around. The kid should have had puddles on his shoulders with how wet he was behind the ears.

It was also about then that I saw Susana's hands curl into fists, thereby signifying that this rookie's life was about to be measured in nanoseconds if I didn't hurry.

"Susana!" I shouted as best I could; my lungs still hurt to pull air in them, but I could at least make a little noise. "Do not kill him!"

That rookie, gods love him, turned to look at me, his mouth working to catch up with his brain, which had finally caught up with the name I had just said. His face went white as the snow around him, an interesting trick for a black guy. "Oh, crap. You're her." It came out as more a wheeze than actual words.

I got to her and gripped her forearms, and I felt the thrumming of anger in them. Her arms were tensed like springs, and she was doing the best she could to keep from unleashing her rage upon a kid who just had the misfortune of not knowing who she was. "Kid, walk. Go get coffee for everyone." I put myself between him and Susana, who seemed to finally start to come down from the rage. "Take your time doing it, too."

"Ohgodohgodohgod…" He backed away slowly a few steps before turning and fleeing as fast as he could without running. Out of the corner of my eye I saw him heading for the local convenience store. Nice to see he could follow orders.

I put my face into Susana's, trying to break her out of the spell she was under. If I wasn't careful, I'd be the focus of her anger. Having had her bounce my head off the ground a couple times over the previous few years, I had no desire to have it happen again. Still, if I didn't calm her down enough, a failed bombing would be the least of my worries.

"You don't have to kill him now. Dead rookies mean paperwork." When I got no response, I took a calculated risk and shook her a little. "Babe, you okay?" I kept my voice low, smiling a bit for her benefit. "Still with me?"

Like a switch, the tension drained from her and tears rolled down her face. "*Jesucristo*, Tommy!" She threw her arms around me and squeezed me tightly, forcing the air from my lungs in a rush. Susana covered my face with kisses. "Are you okay?" She released me and looked in my face.

After gasping a bit, I nodded. "Although I might need a lung transplant after that," I joked.

"You asshole!" Susana beat at my chest, bringing on a whole new bit of pain. "What the hell is wrong with you?"

I tried blocking her blows and failed, which hurt as if she had taken a hammer to my ribcage. "Other than getting beaten up by my wife? My car got blown up."

"I see that, *gringo*." She ceased her assault on me and went back to hugging, though more gently this time. "What happened?"

"Not quite sure yet. Elder's the one in charge here. She's saying the Bomb Squad is still checking it out." I shrugged.

Rika walked over just then, a thin smile on her face. "Hey, Susie Q. How's married life?"

"If I can keep my husband from getting turned into flambé, I'll consider it a win." Susana always used humor and sarcasm to cover when she was upset. Me nearly getting blown up would definitely fall under the category of "Things That Upset The Wife." "What have you got?"

Rika took Susana by the arm, showing her the crime scene, and that's when it all just seemed to hit me. Someone had blown up my vehicle, the car I had nursed and fixed up and treated like a baby. This same someone had decided to either try and kill me in the most flagrant way possible, or wanted to send me a message saying they could get me any time they wanted. Neither thought was very pleasant, and the realization started my hands shaking in a combination of fear and rage. This was not the way things were supposed to go.

I did have to get one thought out of my head. "Larry," I whispered.

"You call, I answer, Thomas." Larry seemed not the least bit concerned for my condition.

"I'm fine, by the way," I growled at him, sore that he wasn't worried about me.

Larry favored me with a raised eyebrow and a quirked-lipped smile. "Of course you are, Thomas. Otherwise, your lovely bride would have lain waste to all that exists, your mother would have done the same, and I would be well on my way to the next Keeper, for all the good it would do, as the world would be a smoldering ruin." Winking at me, Larry continued. "I am rather glad you are still ambulatory, Thomas, if that is any consolation. Life would be quite boring without you."

I couldn't stay mad at him. "Thanks. I need you to do a quick circuit of the place. See if anyone of the Conclave is involved."

The spirit looked at me dubiously. "I will look, but this does not seem like their kind of work. It is not their style, so to speak."

I shrugged and began walking towards the remnants of the Beauty. "Just a look. It doesn't feel that way either, but there's a first time for everything." As I got within a few feet of the charred metal and plastic, I saw a newcomer squatted down on his hunkers using a collapsible pointer to push through some of the debris. His back was to me, though I knew he wasn't part of the local police force by the lack of a jacket saying "POLICE" on the back. The suit coat was of a familiar cut, and the hairstyle was one I had gotten to know in New Orleans. I saw the figure tense as I came closer.

"Mr. Renton?" I said the name hesitantly, in case he wasn't completely sure it was me behind him.

"Tom." The rich voice rolled out my name. Renton stood a couple of inches taller than me, and he definitely worked out a lot more than I did. The suit he wore was all I had ever seen him wear, though this one was a dark grey, and likely wool in deference to the weather. His coat was open, and I saw a flash of the gun under the coat. I knew he had at least three other weapons on him, which made him just slightly less paranoid than my mother. He was her protégé, and with the lantern jaw, the piercing eyes, and the impeccable tailoring, he screamed either movie star or secret agent. "Car trouble?"

"You could say that." It bugged me that I still didn't know the guy's first name. "I didn't see you enter the crime scene."

He chuckled. "Your wife is quite good at distracting people, whether she means to or not." Renton collapsed the pointer and put it in his inside coat pocket. "I've been checking this out and you're not lucky to be alive."

My brain heard the words but didn't capture the importance. I didn't have a chance to ask what he meant when I heard a high-pitched shriek of anger and disbelief.

"Who the hell are you?" Rika stormed over. "What are you doing in a closed crime scene?"

He turned to the newcomer. "You're Rika Elder." Renton said it so matter-of-factly, I almost thought he was reading it off a cue card. "You're the officer in charge here, and third in charge of the Special Crimes Unit for the cities of Hampton and Newport News."

"I know who I am," Rika said, "but that doesn't tell me who the hell you are, and if you have a permit for that piece under your coat."

Renton took a deep breath before releasing it. "I have a permit, Detective, and I am also taking over this investigation."

"What?" Rika and I said in unison.

"Your explosive ordnance disposal team is good for local use, but they missed this." Renton reached into his pocket again and pulled out the pointer. He tapped it against a piece of metal on the ground, twisted and blackened in the heat. "That's a detonator, or what's left of one."

"So?" Rika seemed a bit miffed, not that I could blame her. It's not a good feeling when the Feds take over a case. When the Feds take over a case, they can ride roughshod over an entire investigation, break toes, twist arms, and generally be complete assholes. While that is the exception and not the rule, it only takes one time for bad blood to form.

Thankfully, Renton was not the average Fed.

"Look at it closely." Renton bent over and with a handkerchief picked up the metal. He pointed out a small series of numbers that was mostly intact on one side with his fingernail. "The serial number is from a shipment of radio detonators that went missing three months ago. This is the first time they've turned up."

Rika looked non-plussed. "And how do you know that?"

"I'm with the government, Detective Elder. Just believe me, I know."

"And? I still don't know who the hell you are. For all I know, you may be the bastard who set this up."

"Detective, if I had 'set this up', as you put it, he would be around. Over there, over there, and up there." Renton humorlessly pointed at three spots at random.

Before Rika could fire back, I broke in. "I can vouch for him. His name's Renton. He works for my mom."

"Is that right?" Rika seemed unimpressed. "Doing what?"

"Right now, Detective Elder, making sure that whoever set this bomb off is found." Renton wrapped the cloth around the metal and shoved it into Rika's hands. "Now be a dear and get that over to your EOD people."

From the tone of her voice, I heard Rika look at her hands and roll her neck. "Oh no the hell he didn't!" For those playing along at home, when anyone says that, and especially a woman with a gun, that is an incredibly bad sign. She parted her lips to deliver to Renton a South Memphis can of whoop ass when I shoved into the conversation again. "Mr. Renton, what are you doing here?"

"As I said, Tom, I'm taking over this investigation at the behest of your mother. She has concerns about how the locals might handle things." He turned to walk around the other side of my ruined car.

"No." I laid a hand on his arm.

He stopped instantly and looked at my hand. Though I hadn't put any real pressure on him, it was like he had hit a wall. "No?"

"This was a message to me, wasn't it?"

"What do you mean?"

"I caught what you said earlier, Renton. I was meant to see my car blow up." I looked at Rika, then behind me at Susana who was conferring with a couple of uniformed officers. "Someone nearby wanted me to know they could get me any old time they wanted."

The agent looked to one side then the other before nodding. "In the business, it's called a wake-up call. That doesn't mean the locals can handle it."

"We're pulling the traffic cameras from the stop lights now, Mr. Renton," Rika said. "We considered the possibility someone wanted to see their handiwork and the aftermath." The detective smiled. "We should have it in the next hour or so."

Renton looked impressed. "I suppose that, to get my hands on the footage, I'll have to work with you, Detective Elder?" With a haughty look on her face, she nodded. "Then I will do so," he said, the resignation in his voice mixing with the admiration at the manipulation.

"You'd be surprised at what us locals can do, Renton." The challenge had come back into her voice.

"What's the range on one of those detonators?" I asked.

"A couple hundred yards at most," Renton said. "I prefer detonators with a longer range. These are for those on a budget or want to watch their handiwork."

My eyes scanned the apartment complexes across the street, then discarded the idea. I walked around the back of the Beauty's remains, carefully gauging distances. Taking a deep breath got the stench of burning rubber in my still-tender lungs, which oddly cleared out the cobwebs in my head. I did a slow circle around the wreck and checked off the obvious places it couldn't have been.

In the surrounding area of my office was a convenience store, a strip mini-mall with a pizza place and three apartment complexes across the street. I had discounted the apartment complexes for the simple fact that a strange car in the parking lots would attract notice from the residents. If the guy was as professional as he seemed, he would have thought of that already and made sure that he would be in a place that strange cars were commonplace. That left the mini-mall and the convenience store.

"Line-of-sight only, I take it?" Wheels were turning in my head.

"One of the drawbacks of that particular model." Renton followed my gaze.

That took off the convenience store, and immediately pissed me off. It was bad enough that someone had blown up my car just to get my attention. It was even worse that my body still felt like it had been dragged down the road behind a monster truck over a thousand speed bumps. It was even the penultimate of terrible that my wife whom I loved more than life itself was moved to threaten murder and worse to some poor dumb rookie who didn't know any better for blocking her path.

But setting off a bomb from the parking lot of my favorite pizza place? That is just too cliché.

Chapter Three

Marion's was the best pizza you could find on the Peninsula, bar none. The lady the place was named for had been the wife of the owner, who claimed the recipes came from her. She had been gone for almost twenty years but Luigi still made the pies as she had for the ten years before her death. Their four sons and two daughters worked the restaurant, with the younger two of the boys on the oven with their father, the daughters working the bar and the oldest sons managing the front and the back of the house. Marion's was a fixture like the Hampton Coliseum or Yoder Farm over in Newport News; if Marion's ever went out of business or closed up, it would truly be a sign of the apocalypse.

I'm not kidding. The pizza there is divine.

Having been a regular there for over half a decade, I was on a first name basis with everyone that had anything to do with Marion's. Anthony knew my order the moment I walked in and called it back to Luigi and either Marco or Leonardo, depending on who was working that night. Sonya and Maria would fight over who would serve me the diet soda I would drink as I sat at the bar, waiting for my meal. It was a ritual, one I had done once a week for five years, always on a Friday night.

So it was a bit of a surprise for Anthony to see me walk in on the early evening of a Wednesday, especially considering the fireworks.

"Hey, Mr. Statford!" Anthony greeted me with open arms and a concerned look. Amazingly, he kept a trim form in spite of the amazing food at Marion's. "You okay?"

I nodded, taking in the interior of the restaurant. It had a warm charm, kind of like what people would think of an authentic Italian restaurant. Tables were scattered throughout the main dining area, covered in checkered tablecloths, place settings and condiments. There were rustic chairs, booths against the walls, and just a warm feeling all around. Though I didn't often dine in, it was always a pleasure to do so. It was homey and welcoming, just what a good restaurant should be.

For a Wednesday in the depths of holiday season, it was unsurprisingly empty. Sonia and Maria were at a table wrapping silverware, though that lasted until about three seconds after I walked in. Both girls had run over to me, fluttering their arms and talking a million miles a minute. I assured them both I was just fine over the loud yelling of their brother, who was shouting at them in Italian.

"Folks, I'm okay. Just a little banged up." I had decided to go alone, as Elder was busy trying to keep Renton from taking over the investigation, and Susana was busy trying to keep the two of them from killing each other. "I need to know who was in here about an hour ago."

Sonia looked at Maria, who hung her head in shame. "Some guy with an accent," Maria said quietly.

Anthony rattled off some more Italian before catching himself. "What you mean 'some guy with an accent'? That don't narrow things down for the man!"

Maria fired back. "You were busy in the back with Papa!" She threw one of her hands in the direction of the kitchen while pointing at her brother. "He stopped in, he asked for a beer, he left! If I knew he was such bad news, I'd have handled him myself!"

Sonia jumped in. "Besides, what were you going to do, Tony? Be some big bad guy to the rescue against some guy who just walked in?"

I wish I could say this was a rare occurrence, but the family liked to argue. "Come on, folks," I said. "Knock it off. I just need some information." I might as well have been talking to a wall.

"You think I can't handle things here, Sonia? Is that what you think?" Anthony raised his hands to the ceiling and called upon the Blessed Virgin twice. "If I had seen him, I woulda torn him limb from limb!"

Maria rolled her eyes and started into a blistering tirade against Anthony, which did me no good to try and figure out because it was in Italian. The hand gestures and the tone, though, gave me a great idea of what was being said. "And another thing—"

"Okay, people, that's enough!" I shouted. I don't often lose my temper among friends, but considering the situation, an exception was warranted. All three clammed up instantly. Turning to the youngest sibling, I asked, "Maria, what did he look like?"

"Who? The guy?" She shrugged. "He looked like he wasn't from here. Wasn't dressed for the cold." Maria furrowed her brow, thinking about it deeply. She shoved an errant lock of black hair from her face and brightened. "He was really polite, dressed in a really expensive suit. It looked almost like a tuxedo. We don't see many of those in here."

I nodded. "Okay, you said he had a beer." Maria nodded. "How'd he pay?"

"Cash," Sonia interjected. "He put a twenty down and said to keep the change," Sonia said. "I don't want to sound racist or nothing, but he looked and sounded Mexican."

Usually when you hear those words, someone is being racist. This time, though, it sounded more of a description than anything. "How would you know?" I asked.

"The accent, and we've met a few who come in." Sonia looked a bit shy from the attention, but plowed on with her description. "Dark skin, really thick hair, kinda like your wife." That blew away some of the possibilities. "He just gives off that vibe that he wasn't from around here, and he was definitely speaking Spanish into his phone at the door."

I checked the distance from the register to the door. Fifteen feet in an empty restaurant, no other sounds, a guy not trying to hide his conversation because no one's going to understand him… It was possible. That rather solidified my suspicions and my plans. "Did you hear what he said?"

Sonia shook her head. "I didn't do so hot in Spanish in high school, even if it is just bastardized Italian," she smirked. I was rather glad Susana didn't hear that. "The guy spoke really quick, though, and it wasn't like any Spanish I ever heard. Sorry."

"Thanks, ladies." I smiled, even though part of me wanted to scream in frustration. "If you could work with the cops to get a composite sketch going, I'd appreciate it."

Maria spoke up. "Oh, there's one more thing." She went back behind the bar and dug around a bit. When she came back holding something in a paper towel, she opened the towel up. In her hand was a bright green feather, so green it looked almost like neon paint. "He left this under his mug when he left. I didn't think anything of it until now." Maria looked sheepish. "I like birds, and this is pretty."

I took the feather from her carefully. There wasn't likely to be any good forensic evidence on it, but I wouldn't know until it was checked. "You're awesome, Maria." I was shocked by just how colorful and bright it was, catching the light perfectly. "Thank you. This might help find the guy who blew up my car and almost me in the process."

They offered condolences again and Anthony made me wait for his father to finish a special order for me before I left. Eating was the farthest thing from my mind; I wanted nothing more than to find a deep dark hole that Susana and I could dive into and never come out. There was too much going on and not enough information.

One thing was for sure: I wasn't going to let anyone else be a target.

I carried out the box with one of Mario's special pizzas, the steam coming out of the holes as I made it back to my office. The cops had mostly left, the tapes fluttering in the breeze that had started. The snow wasn't thick as it fell, but it promised to be in the next couple of hours. I made my way over to Rika, who was fuming, and Renton, who might as well have been carved from wood for all the emotion he was showing. Between them was my Susana, giving them both a steely gaze, looking from one to the other with a glare that brooked absolutely zero bullshit. Something told me it was the only way she could keep the two from killing each other, and even then it would be a near thing

I handed over the pie to Rika, who seemed surprised by the maneuver. "The hell is this for?" She lifted the lid and breathed deeply, a smile involuntarily forming on her face.

"That's for you and Renton to eat while you work together." Before Rika could say anything more, I cut her off. "He's got resources you need so deal with it." I rounded on Renton, whose mouth had almost quirked into a smile. "As for you, this lady is one of the best cops out there. She's smart, she's tough as hell, and she knows her business. Do not be a dick." The smirk died on his lips. In my attempt to drive home my point, I came very close to poking him in his chest, but refrained from doing so as I was not completely suicidal. I settled for just pointing at him as threateningly as possible, which wasn't much. "Where's my mom?"

"Unavoidably detained," was the only answer he gave, and the only answer I would get. I may have been the son of super-spy Aveline Statford, and a pretty fair badass in my own right, but from what my mom told me of Renton, he would chew his own tongue off rather than give up any information he wasn't supposed to say. "She sends her love."

My mother was likely hip-deep in some third-world country unleashing hellfire and brimstone upon some poor bastards who had made the mistakes of both pissing off the government of the United States, and getting my mom's agency after them, and she still remembered to say that she loved me. An amazing woman, she had wanted me to get involved in the Agency, but with the calling of the Conclave and position of the Keeper, I declined. "Don't think that being my mom's protégé will get you out of being civil and professional to the local cops."

Renton glanced over at Rika, eyes nearly unreadable beneath the dark glasses. "I can be as civil and professional as she is." The ghost of a smile had returned. "I will do my best."

"Mm-hm." Rika's tone was so full of derision and cynicism, I was surprised it wasn't accompanied by an eyeroll and her hands on her hips. "I'll believe it when I see it, G-Man."

The tall man took his sunglasses off and looked at Rika, a grin forming under his eyes. "Perhaps we got off to a bad start, Detective. I'm Mr. Renton." He held out his empty right hand. "It's a pleasure to meet you, and I do hope we can work together."

Rika narrowed her gaze. "No more secret agent bullshit?" she asked. "One little bit of any 'need-to-know' and I will fuck you up."

"Detective Elder, I have no desire to cause any further issue. Now, that pizza is getting cold and we have work to do." To me, Renton said, "Would it be possible to use your office, Tom?" When I nodded, he gestured toward the door. "I promise to be on my best behavior."

Whether he was sincere or not didn't really matter to me; the slight softening around Rika's eyes was enough sign that she was going for it. I wasn't too worried about the two of them. Even though Rika likely had no formal training in whatever martial arts Renton knew, I had seen her take down a guy in full roid-rage during a domestic dispute, just be hitting him twice. I smiled as I pictured how short the fight would be, and how long it would take the ambulance to get there.

"They look chummy," I heard from behind me, which deflated my happiness that I wouldn't have to explain to my mom why she was short a protégé. Susana wrapped her arms around my midsection, which like the rest of me was starting to get cold. Feeling her warm cheek against my back, I hated myself for what I was about to do, but I knew it had to be done.

"Babe, you need to go."

I felt her stiffen against me at the words. "What?" She released me and turned me around to face her. "Go where?"

My lungs pulled in biting cold air as I weighed my next words. "To Texas," I finally said. "To your father."

Susana pushed against me roughly. "The fuck I do, *gringo*! You can't do this on your own!"

I tried to keep my cool, which was pretty simple in the snow. "I need you there, Susana. I need someone to check something out, and you're the lucky winner."

She stood away from me for a moment. "Why do you think my father would have anything to do with this? He went straight after we got married, remember?"

"You know that, and I know that." I wrapped my arms around myself, shivering in the snow. My coat, though still intact, had been open enough for my body heat to have escaped for the time being. "I don't know if someone didn't get the godsdamned memo about it, though."

"So you think sending me there is going to keep me safe?"

I laughed, more out of self-deprecation than anything else. "Babe, your dad, while no longer the godfather of the Mexican mafia, most likely still has some of the best hired guns on the planet. It'd take an army to get to you."

Susana wasn't convinced. "So why send me away? You need help here. You can't do this by yourself."

"I won't be," I half-lied. Technically, Larry was always with me so I was never alone. "Listen: if this is an out-of-towner, and from what I've got, he sounds from your dad's neck of the woods, I need someone down there who can not only speak the language, but knows the lay of the land." I shrugged my shoulders and gave my best smile. "That's you. I have trouble pronouncing the value menu at Taco Bell."

She gave one last try. "It's Christmas, though! Our first Christmas together. I wanted to wake you up myself."

I shook my head. "Christmas is in a week. I'll have this wrapped up in a few days, you can tell me how awesome Texas is, I can nod my head and disbelieve you, and we can open up our presents at my mom's place like we did last year." My right hand reached out to cup her cheek. "Three days, that's all I'm asking."

Susana kissed my palm and held it between her own hand and her cheek. She closed her eyes and smiled so wide, she got dimples. "Well, I've got a great gift for you, *gringo*. I know you'll love it."

"What is it?"

She took on a haughty air before laughing and pulling herself to me. "You're the private detective. Get to detecting." While she hugged me close, she asked, "How will I know when to come back?"

"You'll know. You'll be back before you know it. Whoever did this isn't trying to be subtle. You know that's when they make mistakes."

Susana looked up at me with her dark obsidian eyes. "I know that you're sending me away for some macho bullshit reason." She smiled. "I'm letting you get away with it because I love you."

"I love you too," I sighed and kissed her. It hurt my heart to have her go, but I knew I would be absolutely worthless finding anyone while she was around. She would be safe; that was all that mattered. Her father's compound (there was no other word for it) was staffed by what seemed to be a small battalion of hard-assed killers. No one on this side of the weirdness would make a play for Susana while she was there.

That left me free to do whatever it took to find a mad bomber. Piece of cake.

Chapter Four

You ever get the feeling that you made a mistake? Not only did you make a mistake, but a huge mistake, one that will haunt you for the rest of your life, however long or short that may be? That was how I felt the night of the eighteenth as I watched Susana's plane taxi down the runway. It took off with no issues or problems into the night, and I felt like that was the last time I would ever see her.

Being a private detective, regardless of my clientele, was never an easy thing. My ass has been kicked rather well whether by mere humans or critters under the thrall of some insane follower of a Babylonian god, so the scars are there. There was always the possibility that I would either come home missing a few pieces or just not at all. I hadn't really thought about the danger and the possible dismemberment until I got married to Susana, and I'd be lying if I said she wasn't the big reason for me to tell the Conclave to piss off. I couldn't allow her to get caught in the crossfire of some god or goddess who was torqued off at me, and since the protection I got didn't extend to family, she was a prime target.

December nineteenth was bitterly cold, in more ways than one. I woke up alone, in the bed Susana and I shared, for the first time in years, the empty side of the mattress seemingly untouched during the night. The wind howled outside, mourning the loss of the night to the sun. I had slept fitfully, with dreams of monsters chasing me through white-tiled halls, the cries of children echoing in my ears, my hands covered in blood. Bits of my nightmare clawed at the back of my mind, making me relive the whole thing again.

All I could do was scream.

All I could see was blood.

All I could taste was despair and rage.

And all my heart could do was beat, keep beating, keep me alive, keep me watching the end of my life. I wept as the leather bindings tore the skin of my wrists, as I felt my shoulders strain and creak from trying to pull free. Blood ran between the bindings and my wrists.

I don't know why I tried to fight, why I bothered. The deed was done. The knife had fallen, and there was nothing I could do about it. Nothing but scream. I woke up just with that scream just behind my teeth. Sweat drenched the sheets as my heart stopped trying to sprint right out of my chest. I exhaled in a gasp, then I inhaled in a hiccough. I licked my lips as if I was thirsty, and my throat felt raw. As I climbed out of bed and made a beeline for the shower, I pondered my moves for the day. The mundane actions of grabbing a pair of underwear and a towel gave me a counterpoint in reality to push the nightmare back into the slasher flick from which it hatched. I started feeling less dreamy and more on solid ground. Real life, such as it was, brought my conscious mind back to where there weren't bloody knives and monsters around every corner.

Bare feet padding across the carpet, I crossed the hall from the bedroom to the bathroom. Unlike some apartment complexes, this one had a full-sized bath along with a shower stall. The second bedroom was pretty much just a game room mixed with a storage room; most of my stuff from the office had made its way to Susana's apartment. I had been put on the lease to make everything legal and neat and tidy. After the little run-in with the godslayer a few years back, the complex had become sticklers for knowing who was staying in their apartments. I didn't much understand the rationale, either, but it was their place, and their rules.

The sense of normalcy the apartment gave me a bit more peace, with its two bedrooms, living room, kitchen with a dining room, and one and a half bathrooms. It restored my equilibrium to turn the knob on my shower, bringing hot water onto my head, knowing that I was in a place of sanctuary from the insanity and cruelty of the outside world. I started to feel more human, more awake.

The hot water washed out the remnants of my dreams and my tiredness. There were very few things that could revitalize me so completely, and a hot shower was one of them. I scrubbed away the memories of the night before, specifically the tears in Susana's eyes as she went past security to the hanger for her father's jet. It took some finagling, but once I explained to Don Salvador what was going on, he made things happen really quickly. The Don was understanding of the situation, and didn't give me a hard time at all, for which I was thankful.

My list of things to do had grown a bit now that I was thinking more clearly. My phone was utterly destroyed in the blast, namely my landing on it, so that was my first stop. After that, I would hit the local cop shop and see just what Rika Elder and Renton discovered. Though it probably would be very little, it was better than nothing. Someone had a real hard-on for me, and I needed to know who.

I stepped out of the shower and reached for the towel.

"To your left, Thomas."

The voice startled me and nearly made me slip in the tub. As it was, I let out a yelp of surprise as I grabbed at whatever I could to stay upright. I slipped and slid and grabbed for the ring holding the towel with my left hand while grabbing the shower curtain with my right. A harrying few seconds later, I felt I was stable enough to shout, "Godsdammit, Larry!"

"Were you expecting someone else?" Larry may have always been by my side, but that didn't mean he couldn't be a smartass on more than one occasion. "I've been calling your name for the past several minutes."

I grabbed my towel and began to dry off. "Sorry. I didn't hear you. I have a lot on my mind."

"Of course you do. As do I."

I stopped for a moment and looked at Larry. I mean, I really looked at him. His usually perfectly styled blonde hair was mussed, and his clothes were rumpled, and not in the fashionable way. There were lines at the sides of his eyes, worry lines, and that never bodes well. "What." It wasn't a question.

Larry tried and failed to look innocent. "What do you mean?"

"You look like you haven't slept in ever."

The spirit's mouth quirked in a tired smile. "I do not sleep, Thomas. You know that."

"No, but you look like shit, and you never look like shit." I pulled on some underwear and continued drying my hair.

Larry cleared his throat, seeming almost embarrassed. "You know me too well, Thomas." He phased through the door before I opened it, then stood at the entrance to the bedroom as I came out of the bathroom. "I am concerned."

"Concerned why?" I tossed the towel on the bed and went to my closet. "This has nothing to do with the Conclave, right?"

"I do not think so."

My back was to him, and the confused tone of voice set my senses on alert. "You don't think so?"

He proceeded into the room, pacing as I dressed in my usual jeans and long shirt. "No one knows anything. It is as if it never happened."

That was when he twitched. Not a little one like when someone gets a small chill, but more like when someone gets an electric shock.

"What was that?" I stopped in the act of putting my wallet in my back pocket.

Larry looked at me dumbfounded. "What was what?"

"You twitched." He started to deny it but I cut him off. "I'm serious. It's like you licked a light socket."

"That is revolting, Thomas, and I did no such thing."

"Dude," I said, "you totally did."

"I most certainly did not."

The hell of it was, I believed him. He didn't know he had shuddered that violently. I decided to let it go for the moment. "So the Conclave is saying that nothing happened."

"They are saying nothing, Thomas." Larry mimed a lean against the wall as I pulled on my shoes. "They act as if they had no idea what I was talking about."

I mulled over Larry's words as I pulled on my shoulder holster and checked my gun. The gods not knowing something was going on wasn't exactly commonplace, but it did happen. This was a bit out of the ordinary, however. Though I had made my feelings about them clear, it would follow logic they would know something about an attempt on me.

That made me pause. Nothing about the attack made sense. I had been caught in the blast, sure, but there was no real danger. Even Renton had dismissed the idea that it was an actual attempt on my life. That left me with the question: why? What was the point of blowing up my car? It didn't make it harder for me to get around, as I was using Susana's Toyota. The blast wasn't even big enough to break any windows; I had only flown through the air because of how close I was.

The idea of flying brought my hand into my coat pocket. The feather was smooth between my fingers, almost like a wisp of smoke, as I pulled it out and unwrapped it from the paper towel Sonia had put around it. It looked so very familiar to me, like from a television show or a book. Though there was nothing to put my finger on, I didn't like the feel of it. The smoke it reminded me of was greasy fumes, like from an oil fire which burned long and low, and seemed to leave some kind of residue on my fingers. I wasn't sure why I hadn't shown it to Rika or Renton, or even Susana when I had the chance. If someone would think to ask, I would tell them it had slipped my mind.

I wrapped the feather and put it away again, this time deeper in my coat pocket than it was before. My real reason for keeping it secret was, admittedly, just my wanting to exact revenge on my own terms. I wish I could say that I held myself to a loftier goal outside of vengeance, but I am, in spite of the beatings I endured over the years and the way I seemed to take a licking and like it, only a mere human, with human thoughts and emotions. Some asshole decided to send me a message. It was only fair that I return the favor.

Grabbing up the keys, I made sure the apartment door was locked before making my way to the car. While the Toyota wasn't exactly my optimal mode of transportation, it did in a pinch, and Susana admittedly enjoyed a few extra horses under the hood than the Beauty. As I cursed because of bending myself lower to get into the car, I whispered Larry into the passenger seat. An idea of where to go was percolating in my brain, and I wanted to bounce the suggestion off my spirit friend.

"You do not have any idea where you wish to go, do you, Thomas?" Larry made a show of stretching out, his upper torso going through the seat while his feet disappeared beneath the floorboard. "You can admit it to me. No one can hear me anyway."

"Believe it or not, I do have a plan." I put the Toyota into reverse after hitting the windshield wipers for the millionth time, finally dislodging the last of the snow.

"I do not," came Larry's sardonic reply.

"Oh ye of little faith!" I smiled. I felt a bit better than I did before, mainly since I was actually doing something instead of brooding. The car went into Drive thanks to the gearshift on the steering column; that would take getting used to. "Whoever did this is connected."

"Granted. Does that improve the odds of finding the mastermind or just make things more difficult?" Larry rolled his eyes as I made my way through the slush out to the highway. "What am I saying? Of course it makes it more difficult."

Thankfully the plows had been through, making the roads only slightly suicidal rather than completely foolish. "I'm betting that feather will give me an idea of what I'm up against."

Larry verbally raised his eyebrow; I was too focused on the road to try and look over at him. "A feather?" The derision in his voice was evident. "Wake up, Thomas! You do realize it is likely from that young lady cleaning up rather than this mystery man, yes?"

I sighed. Larry usually had an edge to his words, but never to this degree. Something was seriously bothering him. Though he had been with a Keeper his entire existence, I knew he was probably one of the loneliest creatures in the world. Maybe my getting married and quitting the job of Keeper had done something to him. "I'm sorry."

"For what, Thomas?" Larry's words were softer, but still possessed of a bite.

"For putting you in the middle of this pissing contest between me and the Conclave. It wasn't my intention."

Larry was silent for a moment, the road bumping slightly under the tires. "What you did was completely throw away a responsibility that has been passed down from one Keeper to the next from antiquity. What the Keeper does is preserve a balance between gods and mortals. When that balance is upset, unfortunate things start happening, and the rest of the mortal world starts to notice." Larry sighed deeply. "Do you know why there are atheists, Thomas?" I shook my head, keeping my eyes on the road but my ears on the conversation. "Some just refuse to believe in anything that cannot be explained. Others refuse because they have seen what mortals have done in the names of their gods, be it Jehovah, Allah, Odin, or others, and it soured them on any belief that involves 'invisible men in the sky'. It is understandable, and unfortunate."

The words dried up from Larry for so long that I said something. "And others?" I prompted.

"The rest refuse to believe that any reality as broken and insane as this one can be ruled by one intelligent being, let alone many. They cannot accept that the entities they call gods can be just as flawed and mistake-prone as they are. As such, they believe that the universe is little more than a happy accident they arrived into screaming and crying and exit a short time later, leaving no mark or trace upon the world at their passing. They simply refuse to believe. "

We drove some more in silence towards Poquoson, a small town on the outskirts of Hampton that had what I needed. It is said that there are two things you never discuss with friends: politics and religion. Larry had no politics to speak of, and our religious discussions mostly centered around the habits and vagaries of the Conclave. I guess I couldn't understand why anyone could not believe in something because I met these gods, or at least enough of them to postulate that the rest of them existed. "That's their choice, Larry. I can't share it because of the things I've seen and the people I've met, but not believing in something is their decision."

"Thomas," Larry said quietly, "have you not seen the world? It is falling apart." His voice rose. "False adherents to the Christ-God's message of love and peace, killing those who refuse to follow their twisted beliefs. Fools who put on vests of explosives to annihilate groups of innocents merely because they are not followers of the Prophet, which goes against the words of Allah. The Inquisition, the Crusades… I could go on, but you get the idea."

"So?" I pulled into the parking lot, thankfully off the roads which began to get slick again in the snow and cold. "In case you hadn't noticed, the world has been going down the crapper for quite a good while."

Larry counted each point off on his fingers. "The words of the Conclave being twisted into mockery. The rise of non-believers in anything. The increase of the believers in the old gods." He looked at me, his gaze piercing my soul. "Now you are refusing to do that which you were chosen. That adds up, Thomas."

"What does it add up to, Larry?"

"Nothing good. Nothing good at all."

"That's pretty godsdamned vague," I muttered as I got out of the car to go inside the building.

From behind me, Larry said, "If you were tired of being constantly misquoted, and constantly ignored, and constantly belittled, would you not take steps to correct that?" He paused for effect. "Especially when you have the power to do so?"

My blood ran colder than the winter I was walking through. That was not a thought or idea I needed running through my skull. Not at all.

Chapter Five

Poquoson is a rather quaint little town, and I use the word quaint in the kindest sense possible. It was not going to be a hustling and bustling metropolis, nor would it be a commercial powerhouse. Poquoson got its nickname "City of One Streetlight" in my youth from the fact that it seemed a lonely town that you'd miss if you blinked while passing through, and the idea of that always stuck with me, even after they got several more. It just always seemed to be the land that time forgot, even though it could be better described as the land that took its time getting where it wanted to go. There were quaint little two-story houses that looked right out of the time of the Cleavers, the only nods to modern times the satellite dish on one side of the roof, the Hyundai in the driveway, the children wearing hot pink jackets as they made snowmen. It was charming without the whole creepy Children of the Corn vibe.

As an added bonus, it has access to some of the best seafood in the Hampton Roads area. Don't ask how, as no one will tell. I know, but I'm not telling.

What Poquoson also had was a top-flight animal hospital, one of the best places to take a pet for anything from vaccinations to tumor removal. I had taken a couple of dogs over the years to Wythe Creek Veterinary Hospital regularly, up until their final trip, and I was on great terms with the vets there. The doctors had a true caring about them, their empathy showing in little ways that added up. When my last dog passed, Dr. Martins let me stay with her until it was over, and offered a box of tissue because of the dusty room. They were fantastic people on whom I could depend, and I knew I would get answers of some kind. Whether they were answers I could use, I would find out soon enough.

The hospital itself was an edifice, though not an imposing one, even in the snowfall. It was painted warm earth colors, with the three stories towering over City Hall, but instead of intimidating, it was inviting and soothing. Murals of dogs chasing balls and sticks competed with painted cats batting at butterflies, combining for a cuteness level enough to send anyone into a diabetic coma. I liked the openness of the place, though, and smiled at the plaque that showed it was funded by the RVF Foundation. The RVF in question had been an animal lover, and donated her fortune to making the Wythe Creek Veterinary Hospital the best of its kind after she passed.

I made my way through the lobby to the waiting room. I was hoping I was at least a little lucky, and my timing was right to miss a bunch of patients and their owners. When I opened the final set of swinging doors, I was greeted first by the scent of animals smacking me in the face, then by a small black and white pug barking ferociously at me. That set off two cocker spaniels, a Labrador, and a Yorkie to announce my arrival with a chorus of woofs and howls. It also made the owners who had brought their cats hold the animals closer in an attempt to keep the felines from freaking out. It mostly worked, but the dogs had to be shushed for several minutes as I held my hands up in surrender and walked carefully to the front desk.

"Tommy!" The nurse greeted me with a warm smile. "It's been forever since you've been here!" She was a sweetheart, blonde, blue-eyed, and filled her scrubs in a matronly way. The aptly-named Nurse Partridge had been a fixture at the hospital for as long as I remembered, and was probably one of the nicest people in general I had the pleasure of knowing. She stood up and walked around the counter for a hug. I wasn't put off; she hugged anyone who loved animals.

I returned the embrace and laughed. "I've been a bit busy, ma'am." I stepped away and held up my left hand, the ring showing.

Her gasp was so loud it got a couple of the smaller dogs yipping again. "And you didn't invite me? I swear, you just wake up and everybody's grown up!" Nurse Partridge fluttered her hands to show her feigned displeasure. "Was it that dear little Mexican girl?"

"Yes, ma'am, it was," I chuckled. Some things you couldn't change. "I was wondering if Dr. Mitchell is around."

"You're a lucky man. She's on lunch right now," the nurse said, heading back behind her desk. After muttering a few words into the telephone, Nurse Partridge sat down again. "She'll be right down."

I nodded my thanks and took a seat as far away from the pug as possible. Not that I was afraid, of course, but because I had no desire to start things up again. Pugs can be vicious little bastards anyway.

After a few minutes, Paula Mitchell, a Doctor of Veterinary Medicine, entered the waiting room. She was statuesque, with fiery red hair pulled back and up, with some loosely falling out of captivity. Her scrubs looked rather lived in, and not for the first time I wondered why everyone didn't wear the things. They're comfortable, disposable, and easy to wear. Of course, they didn't hide weapons that well, nor worked very well when needed as a tourniquet, and also were not that much use in winter weather. Her shoes were the typical soft-soled kind, the ones that real doctors wear because they were on their feet all day, not the fancy kind that get seen on television. Pale skin innocent of makeup, green eyes flashing with intelligence, Paula was a hell of a vet, and a hell of a friend.

"I was wondering when you'd come around, Tom," she said after I rose to give her a hug. "It's too late to get that beagle, but I have a Dobie you might be interested in. Freshly weaned and spayed."

I shook my head, remembering that I was wanting to get a dog for Susana. Though it was too late for a Christmas present, I had plans for her birthday. "It's not about that, Doc. I need some of your book learnin." I drawled the sentence for her amusement.

Half-smiling, Paula beckoned me with a shake of her head. "Talking like that will get you shot around here, Tom."

Following her, I chuckled. "Wouldn't be the first time."

"And it wouldn't be the first time I patched you up." We made our way through the halls to her office. I never really appreciated how big the hospital was until we walked through what seemed to be miles of hallway, past doors marked radiology, examination, serology. The hospital was the largest of its kind in three states, and from the labyrinth we had just passed through, I believed it.

Paula Mitchell's office was lined in bookshelves filled with books, treatises, magazines, and encyclopedias about her chosen profession and potential patients. Her diplomas were on the wall as well, including her graduation from Cornell University as valedictorian. Competing for room were pictures of not only her multitude of pets, ranging from dogs to hamsters to an actual iguana the size of a German Shepard, but grateful patients with their animals she had nursed back to health. Though it should have felt cluttered and claustrophobic, it actually felt comfortable.

"So what brings you here, Tom?" Paula sighed as she sat back in her faux-leather chair. "You don't come here unless it's for one of your insane cases."

"Nothing insane this time, I promise." I reached into the pocket of my coat and pulled out the tissue-wrapped feather. "What kind of bird is this?"

The doctor took the package and unwrapped it carefully. After studying it for a moment, she clucked her tongue. "Where'd you get this?"

"A little bird left it for me," I smiled.

The look of tired pain crossed her face as she regarded me with a glare. "Unless I'm mistaken, it's from a resplendent quetzal. If I remember right, the feathers were used in ancient Mayan ceremonies." She carefully wrapped it again and placed it on the desk. "It's a threatened species, which is why I ask where you got it."

That explained the look of doom she was giving me. "A suspect in a case left it behind. I'm trying to find out what I can about it so I can figure out who did it."

Paula leaned back in her chair. "Did 'it'? Did what, Tom?"

Crap. Me and my big mouth.

"Well, you see, someone blew up my car, likely the one who had that feather." Paula's mouth opened in shock. I held up a hand to forestall any questions. "The girl who found it fished it out of the garbage, so there wasn't likely any forensic evidence on it. The cops have a bunch of other evidence from the blast; this is just something that bothered me and I wanted to check it out."

"Were you hurt?"

"Just got singed a little." I took the bundle and put it back in my pocket. "Scared the hell out of me more than anything." While that wasn't the whole truth, it was enough to mollify the doctor. "Really made Susana mad."

"That's right," Paula smiled. "I heard she made an honest man out of you. She's not someone I would want mad at me."

I nodded. "I have her checking something out far away from here. No need for her to get caught up in something about me." Standing, I offered my hand to the doctor. "Thanks for your time, Doc. I thought it would be more, but not every lead can pan out."

She stood and took my hand, squeezing it gently. "Try not to be such a stranger, Tom. I'm still looking for that dog for you."

That made me smile. "Thanks." I remembered roughly how to get back to the parking lot, cursing myself for wasting time. I ended up wasting even more time getting outside, after asking for directions twice and still making two wrong turns. The automatic glass doors opened to the biting wind that had picked up quite a bit, sending swirling snow twisters across the white-covered asphalt. I pulled my coat tight around me, trying to put the waste of time out of my head.

Was I chasing shadows, trying to make this more than it really was? The thought crossed my mind as my right hand dug into my pocket for my keys. Sure, this wasn't the first time someone had come after me personally, but the feeling was not something anyone really wanted to get used to having. To mangle an old saying, just because you're paranoid doesn't mean they're out to get you. The universe, though I was loathe to admit it, did not necessarily revolve around me. It could have just been a one-and-done attack, or even a mistake. While Chevy Trackers weren't in every driveway, I had seen a few going up and down the road. The more I thought about it, the more likely it seemed to be more a mistake or one-time thing. It made more sense than thinking someone was coming directly after me, and I had halfway convinced myself of that as I pulled out my keys and looked for a chunk of red in a sea of white.

That was when I saw someone on the ground beside the Toyota, his left arm all the way under the car.

I was about thirty feet away as the guy took a quick look at me, shimmied out from under the Toyota, and sprang to his feet. My mind reacted before the rest of me, taking in the thick, coarse hair, the black tuxedo jacket, the dark skin, and sent me after him at a dead run. He had about a five-step lead to start, but I wasn't about to let him get away.

The parking lot had been somewhat filled with cars, and this guy ran between tightly parked SUVs and minivans, moving like liquid smoke around the huge vehicles. I wasn't so lucky, banging my shoulder into a Dodge Caravan and grabbing blindly at a side mirror as I tried not to faceplant and lose the son of a bitch. I let out of a cry of pain when I left a couple of strips of skin from my hand on the metal. My keys fell to the ground, the metal lost under the drifting white stuff. I could see the bloody handprint I left on the Caravan as I pushed myself after him.

He ran toward the turn entrance to the hospital that was on Little Florida Road, one of the two main drags into Poquoson. Cars and trucks zipped by, unmindful of the weather as they usually were, going at least ten above the posted limit of forty-five. If he kept going another fifty feet, he would get creamed, and I would lose any answers I might find. I screamed at him to stop, my arms pumping as I raced after him. To my shock, he did just that, skidding in the snow and ice. I pinwheeled my arms to try and keep my balance, managing it only by the skin of my teeth. My hand went under my coat and grabbed my gun. I was thankful for the checkerboard grip because of the blood on my hand, and I pointed it at the guy, now only a dozen feet away.

"Who the fuck are you?" I shouted. "What do you want?"

He said nothing as he turned around and raised his hands, and I got a good look at him. He looked normal, save for the tuxedo in a snowstorm. The guy looked anything but uncomfortable, as he was not shivering or shaking, while it took a conscious act of will to keep the barrel of my pistol trained on him. His face was angular, his nose and cheekbones almost forming a perfect T. His eyes were black disks surrounded in white; I don't mean they were a dark brown or anything, I mean black, as if the pupil was the entire iris. I even think I stepped back a bit, as I usually only saw something like that when I was dealing with my side of the weirdness.

"Who are you? Answer me!" I might as well have been yelling at stone. "Why are you after me?" Still no words, but his right hand reached under his coat. "Whatever that is, take it out nice and easy, pal!"

He took it out, "it" being a grey-bladed knife with no hilt. The blade itself was only about four inches long and looked hewn out of rock. The knife looked brand new, though it felt ancient. I felt just pure antiquity dripping off of it as he slowly brought the knife above his head and held it with both hands.

"Put the knife down, asshole." Though I usually shot one-handed, I brought my left hand to cup my right, taking what was known as a Weaver stance. The cold was starting to get to me. "I'm not going to warn you again."

His mouth started to move, whether finally deferring to the cold or some kind of prayer. He interlaced his fingers, and I saw his arms tensing. I almost couldn't believe it. He was actually going to come at a guy aiming a gun at him, armed with just a knife. I resolved to just shoot him in the kneecap.

"You might want to rethink that, buddy," I said as I lowered the gun to take careful aim at his right knee. If he kept coming, I'd blow out the left one, too. My patience was wearing thin. "Put the godsdamned knife down."

I had just decided to shoot the knife from his hands when he let out a horrible yell, one that started from what seemed like the bottom of his soul. There was a Power in his cry, one that was usually reserved for the gods or demigods. I took an involuntary step back, not from the force of the cry, but the shock of hearing one like it come from a seemingly mortal throat. I heard glass shatter behind me, which made me take a step forward.

When he was done, he looked at the sky and said something. I could barely hear it, let alone understand it, but I focused on the way his lips moved and formed the words so I could replay it in my head. After that, he looked at me, his obsidian eyes boring into me. His body visibly relaxed, as if his scream let out every care and sin he had ever held, and he was finally free. He smiled at me, the kind that one gives when communicating a great secret.

I watched him plunge the knife into his own chest. And he kept smiling.

Blood spurted from the wound, though not that far since his hands blocked the flow. The blood back-spattered onto his face, giving him a crimson-speckled mask. Somehow, he had enough presence of mind to twist the knife, enhancing what was already a fatal wound, but his expression never changed. The man fell, first to his knees, then pitching forward onto his face, finally hiding that hellish smile. He tensed one last time, then died, kneeling in front of me as if he was in prayer.

I lowered my gun, holding it in my own bloody right hand. My mouth was dry, and I knew my eyes were wide in horror. I had never seen anything like that in my life. Sure, I had seen sharp nasty pointy things go into people, sometimes even all the way through people, but not a Mexican version of seppuku. That was a bit much, even for me.

Getting as close to the body as possible without stepping in the bloody snow and slush, I saw the blood wasn't pooling out from around the corpse. Knowing I had to make sure he was dead, I steeled myself as I placed my foot against his left flank and pushed hard. When he didn't move, I braced myself and did it again. It took a good heave but he fell onto his right side.

The knife had gone clear through the white dress shirt and split skin and broken bone with a sickening, frightening ease. The tensing he did while hunched over had likely been him breaking open the rib cage to allow the heart to spill out, as it had been sliced free of the aorta. The cut was clean, almost surgical, and the organ no longer beat. It just laid there, steam coming off it in the cold. The lungs were damaged rather badly with the impromptu surgery, the pink tissue showing where the blade had done its work to get the heart out. I covered my mouth from the sheer clinical brutality of it, then looked at his face.

He was still smiling.

Chapter Six

I'm not sure how long I stood over the grinning corpse, but it couldn't have been more than a few seconds. I replayed the incident in my mind, trying to figure out how things had gone so wrong. Putting my gun under my coat, I walked away briskly towards the hospital. Though it was both too late for the guy and the wrong kind of hospital anyway, I could at least try and preserve some kind of evidence for the cops when they arrived.

All the while, inside my head, two people were talking to me. One was the yammering voice that showed up every time I saw something that defied logic and sanity; we were well-acquainted. It gibbered and whined and cried and decided to put all the best and bloodiest scenes on display in full IMAX on my brain. I saw the knife go in with no resistance, sliding through the ribs with no issue. It showed me the smile, over and over again, pointing out that it was a really sick puppy who would grin while gutting himself.

That was when the other voice sighed and patiently explained that he did not gut himself. This staid, stately voice explained in excruciating detail that, if it was a gutting, there would be intestines and bowels and other parts of the lower gastro-intestinal tract. There also would not have been such an arterial spray at the first strike. This dignified voice that sounded completely upper-class British went on that there was something more important than how the guy snuffed himself.

Of course, I'm telling both of these voices to shut up for a minute so I can keep from throwing up. Naturally, neither listened. In fact, the rational voice kept saying I needed to listen to him, and I silently said I would, as soon as I could get my bearings.

Not me, you idiot, said the reasonable voice. *Him.*

As I made my way back through the parking lot, leaning my uninjured left hand on cars and trucks to keep my balance while I searched for my keys, I mumbled Larry's name. He appeared instantly, which made me feel much better.

"Oh my, Thomas," he said in greeting. "Did you lose him?"

I cursed myself for a fool for not allowing Larry to roam freely. He could have followed the guy easily, and I could have found him at any time. Things were happening too weirdly and too quickly. "He lost himself. Stone knife through the chest." Near the Caravan, I saw a glimmer of metal in a small hole. I breathed a sigh of relief as I picked up the keys. As I got to the Toyota, I laid down in the snow furrow the dead man made while under the car. "Pretty messy."

"I thought you did not use knives."

A quick check under the car revealed nothing explosive or out of the ordinary, at least as far as I could see. "Oh you're frigging hilarious. It was his own knife."

"You took it from him?"

I pulled myself off the ground, cold and wet and getting agitated. "No, he carved his own heart out himself." Larry winced in sympathy. "Yeah, so my fun meter has gone from pegged to buried the godsdamned needle, and I'm no closer to figuring out what the fuck is going on. I'm starting to get a bit miffed, Larry."

"I can certainly understand that, Thomas," Larry nodded. "I wish I could shed some light on matters."

"So do I." I unlocked the car door and sat inside, not turning on the engine quite yet. I was missing something yet again.

"Did he say anything before he took his own life?"

I shrugged, my mind not really firing on all pistons. "I dunno. He was mumbling something under his breath." The wind blew across the parking lot, swirls of snow and ice forming twisters over the relatively empty lot. "A prayer for the dying, maybe?"

"I do not know what it could be, Thomas, if I do not know the words."

This is where you were supposed to pay attention, the British brain-voice said, disapproval dripping from each word.

"I can't remember it all," I said.

A smirk was on Larry's face. "You cannot remember words spoken only a few moments ago, yet you are able to recall ridiculous jokes from a British comedy troupe *en toto*?" A snort of disgust escaped the spirit. "With the correct accents and inflections, I might add."

Listen to the words, the voice whispered. See the words on the lips.

"Gimme a second." My eyes closing, I pictured the scene in my head, trying to capture everything with my mind's eye. The wind was cold, but I pushed that out of thought, trying to only feel the cold that I felt a few moments before. I stopped feeling the wet from the slush and only the crystals on my face. My gun was pointed at his chest, where a knife would appear in only a moment. The shot would have been easy, even easier than at the range.

You're looking at the wrong moment, idiot.

I rewound time, slowly enough that I could tell where I wanted to start again.

A little more, the maddeningly calm voice ordered, and you'll see it.

From the beginning: He stopped. He didn't have to stop, but he did. He couldn't have known for sure I could put a bullet through the knee and put his ass on the ground, but he stopped anyway. That meant he knew exactly who I was and what I could do.

A good start, idiot. Keep going.

He was smiling as he turned around. Smiling like he was in on a joke and I wasn't. Like he knew something I didn't.

I felt a mental smack to the back of my head. Not quite. Try again. Idiot.

Like he had been expecting me. Like he wanted to be caught.

Better. Much better. Go on.

I vaguely heard Larry say something but I pushed it away. I was getting close to something. To my inner voice, the one not gibbering in fear, I pointed out that if the walking dead man wanted to get caught, why did he kill himself?

Listen.

I am listening, you son of a bitch.

The smack again. Not to me, you godsdamned idiot. To him.

I focused on the man's lips as he pulled the knife from his jacket. It was a practiced motion, not unlike watching someone pull out their wallet at a restaurant. I felt the smack on my mental head again and a hiss to listen to him. Some of it was garbled. In fact, a lot of it was garbled. I couldn't understand a single thing said.

You don't have to understand, idiot. Just remember it. What did he say?

My mouth formed the words I saw, and I pushed air through my throat and mouth to make the sounds. I tried to let it come out naturally, the way the dead man did. Each word sounded alien to my ears.

"Et. Keek. Ha kneel. Pa eek. Pock. Ka awn." I waited for the inevitable mental smack, but this time it didn't come.

Close enough, Keeper. Close enough. Now, open your eyes.

"What did you say, Thomas?" Larry was bent over, looking me in the face with concern etched in his brow. When I repeated it, he grew more agitated. "Where did you hear that?"

"From him just before he offed himself. What does it mean?"

"It is from a language that barely a million people speak today. It translates roughly to 'With innocent blood falls the walls of heaven.' It is not a language I have heard often, or recently."

My mind focused on two of the words. "What does that mean, 'innocent blood'? Whose blood?"

Larry stood up abruptly and shook his head. "I do not know, Thomas. There are a great many possibilities."

My brain locked on to only one. Two possibilities, as a matter of fact. I slammed the door to the Toyota closed and gunned the engine. "Get in the car!" Skidding out of the parking space, I sped to the other exit from the hospital, onto Wythe Creek Road. I gave the stop sign a quick glance as I whipped my eyes to the left. Even if there had been a parade coming, I wouldn't have hesitated. The accelerator went down as I gave the wheel a vicious turn to the right, making the Toyota fishtail in the ice and sludge on the road. Even with the sun fully up, there was a constant freeze going on with the wind.

Larry sat next to me, though I couldn't give him a split-second of attention. As treacherous as the roads were, I needed all my concentration. That didn't stop him from talking. "Where are we going, and will we make it in one piece?"

"You might," I grunted through grinding teeth. "Those fuckers."

"What is it, Thomas?"

"Those bastards. They want to hurt me." I juked the car to the left lane, the engine groaning in protest as I redlined the tachometer.

I could hear the dawning of comprehension in Larry's voice. "They could have killed you at any time."

My hand laid down on the horn, trying to get people the hell out of the way. I swung the car onto Commander Shepard Boulevard at about twenty miles over the posted limit and climbing. "They aren't trying to kill me. They're trying to hurt me, and what's the best way to hurt me."

"Are you able to call them?" Larry began wringing his hands.

"I didn't get my phone fixed yet," I snarled, pulling the useless device from inside my coat and throwing it to the floorboard. "I can't even get the damned thing to turn on!"

"Drive faster, Thomas." From the corner of my eye, I could see Larry leaning forward. "You must drive faster."

"If I could get these dumbasses out of my way, I would!" I saw traffic start to snarl up the closer I got to the military base. "Oh fuck me!" I slammed my hand onto the wheel in frustration, the blow going all the way up my arm. "Move, you stupid bastards!" I screamed as I held down the horn. "Move, godsdammit!"

You're forgetting something, idiot. That mental smack again. Whoever that was in my head was an even bigger asshole than I was.

"Thomas, are you not forgetting something?" Larry said, his voice raised to get heard over my screaming.

As my speed dropped from fifty to thirty, I slammed my hand on the wheel again. Of all the times for people to be getting in the way of my driving, it couldn't have been worse. I wished I was in the Beauty, as I knew I could snake around these people, which wasn't even possible in a Toyota. While not an off-road vehicle, a Tracker could make it much easier than the piece of shit I was driving. Susana just had to drive a Toyota Camry, which was good for a police car, but not much else. A Camry had difficulty with potholes the size of quarters, and---

A police car. It finally registered. I gave myself a mental smack to the head.

I hit the lights and siren, hearing the warble starting from outside. The cars in front of me began to part like the Red Sea, which suited me fine while I pushed through. I blared the horn again at some jacked-up truck that had wheels taller than my car who wasn't moving fast enough. My tires caught a bit of traction on the road as I floored the accelerator, jerking the wheel savagely to the right. I didn't even think to waste time with giving the dumbass in the truck the finger.

The speedometer crested ninety as I raced down Magruder Boulevard making the sharp left turn with nothing but luck and a scream of rubber from the tires. Even as frantic as I was, I had chosen my path for maximum speed and minimum obstacles. The lights and sirens definitely helped, forcing people to get the hell out of my way. I managed not to cause at least three accidents, with only a coat of paint separating me from each catastrophe.

Blowing through two stoplights as I headed for the interstate, I cursed myself for a fool. I should have seen it earlier, and I hadn't because I was too focused on fooling around and chasing pointless leads for one reason or another. If I had been thinking like a detective should, I would have realized exactly what their plan was, and skipped going to a godsdamned veterinary hospital. If I had been smart, I would have loaded up and let them come to me, and I would have had all the advantages.

Yeah, and if Hera had balls, she'd be twice the man Zeus was.

Bits started to add up to a picture that I had no desire to see. My exit came up quickly and took it as if all the demons of all the hells were after me. Perhaps they even were; I didn't care. I was no more than four miles away, making me four minutes from my destination the way I was driving. On my left was my office, the police tape fluttering in the wind, the remains of the Black Beauty covered by a blue tarp. I barely gave it any thought as two more lights were passed, and, with the Toyota screaming like a banshee and lit up like a madman's idea of Christmas, I tore the wheel to the right. I took the turn so hard even Larry gasped in surprise.

Godsdammit, if anything happened, I swore I would hunt down each and every one of those motherfuckers and slit their throats.

Another hard left, and my foot barely touched the brake before flooring the accelerator again. Two more miles and no more than one hundred seconds.

The heavy storms before Christmas had caused schools to close, which was fine by the kids, and even more by the parents who could go to warmer climates for the winter. What that translated to was my being able to roar past two elementary schools at twice the posted limit with no real worry about hitting anyone. I counted myself lucky again as I stayed in the middle of the road, giving myself enough room and time on both sides to make any drastic maneuvers. Trucks had already been through, salting the roads and vainly melting the ice. Plumes of slush intermittently splashed to either side.

Forty seconds.

I pulled my gun from my coat and put it in the console, the grip still covered with blood. I fishtailed twice with another quick turn, the second to last. A scream ripped from my throat as I regained control and gunned the engine again. The car flew into the air as it hit a speed bump, sending my head into the ceiling. Stars flew across my field of vision as I struggled to maintain control. Wrenching the wheel savagely, I saw my destination.

I spun out in front of my mom's house and flung the gear shift into Park. Throwing the car door open with my left hand, I gripped up my gun with my right and stalked up the walk. I wasn't trying for a stealth entrance; the sirens and lights along with the screaming tires and roaring engine announced my arrival better than anything. I was going for pure shock value: hit fast, hit hard, hit them until they were down and not getting back up.

A brief flash came across from the calm part of my brain. Leave one alive to get answers about where this was all coming from, Keeper.

I'll take it under advisement, I mentally snarled as I kicked the door in. The wood split easily thanks to knowing where to kick and the metric ass-tons of adrenalin coursing through my body. I raised my gun to defend against any possible ambushers near the front door. Seeing none, I made my way farther through the house to the living room, first checking the hall to my left and the dining room to my right. A quick glance up the stairs showed my mom's room shut and locked tight, as it would be since she was out of the country.

I knew the house well, having spent time there when my office had to be fumigated, or the dogs had needed to be watched, or any number of things that got me coming home. Pictures lined the walls, mostly of family. There were also some landscapes of places I knew she had been, where I thought she had been, and where she flatly denied ever setting foot. The entire place was tastefully decorated, using every trick and method that was on the home decorating shows, and a few she had come up with herself. My mom may make James Bond look like Mr. Bean, but she could make any house into a home with a few knickknacks and throw pillows.

That made things even worse. Knowing some human monsters had invaded this place that was the center of my universe with murder on their minds made my blood boil. There was no place in all the world these bastards could hide from me if they laid even a glance on the two innocents.

"Hannah! Jacob!" I shouted, lowering my gun against my leg. I was too keyed up and needed the extra half-second of decision time bringing up the weapon to decide friend or foe. "Come on out!"

They weren't in the living room.

The dining room, either.

The family room was empty. To say I was beginning to panic would be an understatement. A sofa, a table, and a chair were placed properly, with a television on the wall. The television was off, as was the DVD player and video game system. Three cups of cocoa were on the low coffee table, which proved to be somewhat hot after a quick check. That sent my mind into overdrive as I reasoned the kids were still there.

Something else tripped my mind. Three cups. My brother-in-law and my sister hated cocoa. They would drink eggnog or whatever latte concoction they got from the local Starbucks, but they wouldn't touch chocolate. I looked closely at the areas around the cups and saw something bright green peeking out from between the sofa cushions. I pinched the thing between the fingers of my left hand and pulled it free.

A feather. A bright green godsdamned feather. Fuck.

Behind me, I heard the sliding glass door to the backyard open, with the babbling of two short people who were near and dear to my heart, with another voice mixed in, one I didn't recognize. I flung myself through the entrance of the family room with a standing jump, my gun up and my finger on the bangswitch.

"Get the fuck away from them!" I screamed, catching myself with a hand on the doorjamb.

My scream was met by three screams in return as my eyes took in the pitiful scene of my niece and nephew being shoved behind a fourteen-year-old girl I finally recognized as Marcy Nesbit, their babysitter. The barrel of my Beretta was no more than three feet from her forehead, my finger no more than three ounces of pressure from pulling the trigger.

Marcy covered both Hannah and Jacob as best she could, babbling incoherently to not hurt them, to take her, to not be a monster. The denim jacket she wore sported a couple of lines of feathers, some of them bright green. She then reached for a nearby plant and swung it at me while telling the kids to run.

Gods, that girl was brave. Not even a hundred pounds soaking wet and she was like a momma bear with her cubs.

I caught the plant with my free hand and hit the safety on my gun. She pulled the soon-to-be destroyed flower out of the pot and started hitting me with it. I sputtered between strikes, trying to calm her down. "Marcy, it's me! Tom!"

"Leave them alone!" she screamed. "They're just kids!"

"Godsdammit, Marcy, knock it off!" I grabbed her hand and shook her lightly. "It's me!"

"Uncle Tommy!" I heard Hannah squeal. "Don't hurt Marcy! She wasn't being mean." Jacob echoed her statements, his thin voice high in excitement. They ran to grab my legs in a bearhug apiece, trying to pull me away. Wails started from both of them.

Lovely. Now my niece and nephew thought I was going to kick a teenager's ass. And now for my next trick: kicking a puppy.

The words of the kids seemed to bring Marcy out of whatever attack mode she was in. Recognition dawned in her eyes as she stammered, "Mr. Statford?"

I put a smile on so fake it might as well have read Made In Taiwan. "Yeah, it's me. It's okay."

"What are you doing here?" Marcy said, tears falling from her eyes. "Why are you pointing a gun at me?

To say I felt like Mister Supreme Asshole was an understatement. "I thought something was going on. I'm sorry I scared you all---"

That was the point where things went from terrible to completely irrevocably horrible.

"Drop the gun!" The authoritative shout came from the doorway.

You remember the doorway, idiot? the voice inside my head tutted. The one you kicked down? Where outside you left a cop car running with sirens blazing?

I raised my hands in an all-too-familiar way. "Stay cool, officer. I'm family."

"Don't you hurt my uncle!" I felt Hannah let go of my leg and run behind me. I twisted my neck enough to see my niece kick one of the uniformed cops in the shin. Jacob took it upon himself to go after the guy's partner.

"I'll kick your butt!" Jacob screamed as he hit the cop in the stomach. Having been punched there by Jacob, the kid had a hell of an arm.

I closed my eyes tightly, and the words escaped my mind before I could stop them.

At least it can't get any worse.

"What the hell is going on here?" Jennifer Gage, my sister, yelled as she walked into the living room.

It was at that point I almost asked the cop to just shoot me. It would have been kinder and quicker.

Chapter Seven

One of the things I have learned over my career that has saved my hide more times than I can count isn't my skill with a gun. It isn't my driving skills, which leave much to be desired. It is also definitely not my acting and blending abilities that anyone will tell you are nigh-nonexistent. It isn't even my ability to take more punishment than a piñata at a Little League game and keep on trucking.

The thing I have learned is patience.

You see, everyone thinks that private detectives go through their careers, gun in one hand, dame in the other, beating up the bad guys without a sweat and foolishly rushing in where wise men run the hell away. I mean, sure, that has happened to me a few times, but those are the exception rather than the rule. Most of my cases are spent sitting in a car or seedy hotel room waiting for someone to show up, or waiting for some information in an email or a phone call. Sometimes, I might have to wait for days. Without regularly exercising the virtue of patience, I would most likely have been a smear on the ground years before.

I had outwaited mob bosses, assassins, gods, and demons. I even sat still as a stone in my office for nearly an hour as pushy religious people tried without success to get me to come to the door to let them in. To say that I waited a long time to finally ask Susana to marry me wasn't altogether untrue; I just made sure it was the right time.

It was from this wellspring of nearly-Zen Master endurance I drew as my sister unloaded both barrels on me in a constant barrage. Arthur Gage had taken Marcy home and was taking care of the kids while Jennifer verbally tore me a new one. By the count in my head, the screaming was in its fifteenth minute, and I lost count of the number of times she called me stupid. The f-bomb was also dropped repeatedly. There was also the hollering about how the kids were endangered by my actions, and how I was a complete asshole for pointing a loaded gun at a fourteen-year-old, and I was lucky that Marcy and more importantly her parents weren't going to sue the living shit out of me for reckless endangerment, and on and on.

Being that my sister was a lawyer, and more specifically my lawyer, I took what she said seriously. The problem was all her questions were rhetorical, and circled back to calling me a stupid asshole. When I tried to agree with her, she silenced me with another blast of words. I did little more than sit there and accept the berating. After all, I felt I deserved everything she said and more.

Most people by the fifth minute would have gotten up and walked out. I was made of sterner stuff than that. I could take a hell of a lot more than she could dish out, and what was more, I agreed with her. She was absolutely right about every single word. As such, I would not be walking out on her diatribe.

Granted, the handcuffs were what really made it impossible, along with sitting at a table in an interrogation room at the Newport News/Hampton Joint Police Center. They frown on folks releasing themselves.

I was brought in on improper use of a police vehicle, speeding, reckless driving, breaking and entering, possession of a firearm, and two counts of assault on a police officer. Yes, they rolled the kids attacking the cops onto me, as if that was my fault. Technically, it was, but at that point, it was beside the point. I was starting to run out of things to count in the room to keep my temper in check. Even I have my limits.

"What in the hell is wrong with you?" my sister screamed again. "Those are my children, and you bring a gun into Mom's house! They could have gotten hurt!"

I said nothing and counted to ten before she started up again. Speaking would do nothing but upset her further, and I needed to keep in her good graces so she could bail me out.

"You are in such deep shit I can't begin to even tell you." Jennifer opened my file and exhaled heavily. "I have half a mind to just leave you here. You need to cool off, and maybe taking the heat for these charges will wake you up."

That got my attention. "Wake me up?" I was incredulous. "Did you see what I drove to the house? You know why I'm driving it?"

Jennifer shrugged as she sat down across from me. "That's not the point, Tommy. You were driving like a maniac. You could have killed dozens of people, not including Marcy Nesbit!"

"I didn't kill anyone. I had to get to the house because---"

"Someone was coming after the children?" Jennifer scoffed. "Tommy, there's no reason anyone would want to go after Hannah and Jacob. They could have gotten to the panic room before anything happened. You put a lot of people in danger over a feeling? That's just stupid."

Being called stupid was starting to grate on me. "Okay, what about the guy who cut his own heart out in Poquoson?" I leaned forward in the chair, the chains clinking with the movement. "He said that with innocent blood the walls of heaven would fall. Are you telling me I shouldn't react to that?"

Jennifer looked at the mirror on the wall, which I knew had cops behind it, and likely a police shrink. "About that. The police went to the spot you indicated. They didn't find a body." I opened my mouth to say something, but she silenced me with a gesture. "The only thing that corroborates your story is the blood they found. You owe Harley big time."

Harley was a full-blood Seneca Indian, and the chief medical examiner and forensics guy for the Hampton/Newport News area. Normally, it would be at least two or three separate people who had those jobs, but Harley was damned good at all of it, so they just gave him the positions. "So that means there's likely someone else out there," I said. "Probably at least three others. Do you blame me for doing what I did?"

She sighed deeply, emotions warring on her face. Jennifer was a hell of an attorney, but a terrible card-player. "Can I blame you? No. Can the city blame you?" She shrugged. "Probably. They'll try like hell to get you on the traffic stuff at the very least." Jennifer leaned forward. "Do you realize how serious this is?" she hissed. "You're not getting hit by the Feds only because it's Mom's house and you're her son. You're supposed to think clearer than that! Why didn't you call someone?"

"My phone is still busted," I deadpanned. "You know, from that explosion yesterday?"

Jennifer drew back a bit from that. "Okay, fine."

"Besides, any cop who didn't see another unit racing like the wind down I-64 and think something might be wrong doesn't deserve his frigging badge. I had a plan."

"Bullshit, Tommy." The words were flat. "You were making it up as you go along. Dammit, you still are! You just wanted to solve everyone's problems by yourself. Again."

That stung. "Am I under arrest, Counselor?" My words came through clenched teeth.

"No, surprisingly." She packed up the folder and stood. "Because of your status as a consultant and the extenuating circumstances, the police are going to drop any charges."

I sat up at that. "Thank you."

The disappointment in my sister's voice was a solid thing, blanketing her words in sadness. "Don't thank me. I told them you needed at least a night in jail to pull yourself together." My jaw dropped in surprise. "I love you, Tommy, but you know how much my babies mean to me. Get all this behind you before you come back."

And with that, my sister walked out on me, and by extension my niece and nephew. Cold anger filled me as I sat alone in the interrogation room. My head bowed and my eyes closed as I went into a simmer. It wasn't anger at my sister, but at myself. She had been right on every note. I could have called someone, anyone, while I was on the way to my mom's place. Susana's Toyota had a radio in it; a call would have taken only a few seconds. I had very nearly gone in with guns blazing, and I likely would have shot an innocent girl.

I heard the door open. "You did what you thought was right. No one can fault you for that." Renton stopped where my sister had sat.

I nodded at the words, but couldn't bring myself to believe them. "Any luck?"

"In a minute. Let me unlock you." I felt his hands on my wrists, unlocking the cuffs and letting them fall to the table. My own hands went to my wrists, rubbing circulation back into them. I looked up at him and he had a rare half-smile on his face, as well as the ever-present sunglasses. "There. Now we can get back to work. Come on."

I stood up and followed Renton out of the room. We made our way through the labyrinth of a police station, Renton leading the way, me trying to wrap my head around how so much had gone wrong so quickly. Things were happening too fast, and I was still trying to play catch-up. Going over the few facts I had didn't help matters at all. I pulled back from thinking about what I knew, or thought I knew, for the moment. I was too close to it, and some other perspectives would help.

When we reached Rika Elder's office, Renton opened the door and walked in. I followed, and was amused as always by the state of Rika and her office. It could be described best as controlled chaos. Case notes were pinned, taped, stapled and in one case letter-openered to the cork-covered wall opposite the door. To my right as I walked in was her desk, with mountains of papers and a trio of computer monitors competing with a keyboard and four coffee mugs, each with a varying amount in them, for real estate. The wall opposite from her desk had a huge monitor with multiple feeds on it, one of which was the interrogation room I had just left. The lights were low, which suited me fine. I never understood the corporate love affair with blazing overhead lights, but Rika hated the things with a passion.

Rika looked up from her middle monitor as we walked in, raising up a bit to see over a pile of paperwork. Her eyes lit on me, images reflected in her glasses. "You're an asshole, Statford."

I chuckled dryly and shrugged my shoulders. "That seems to be the assessment going around about me these days."

Renton went to the cork wall, seemingly engrossed in reading the notes. "You kept something back from us, Tom."

I closed the door behind me and leaned on the jamb. "It was a feather. I didn't even know it was a big deal." I was being defensive and I knew it. I was also not being completely truthful, and I knew that.

Of course, so did they. "Bullshit, Tommy," Rika said. "Someone comes after you and you're treating it like one of your crazy cases. This is a bombing. A plain old run of the mill bombing."

"Rika's right, Tom." Renton turned around, his hands behind his back. "This isn't just your problem. You have resources. Use them."

"You know, if I wanted people to yell at me, I'd have kept talking to my sister." I pushed away from the door and walked to the big monitor. The feeds included central processing where they booked people, the holding cells, the drunk tank, and the interrogation rooms. "I'm sure you both saw her verbally beating the hell out of me?"

"While I disagree with her assessments on your intelligence, Tom, she is right about you trying to save the world by yourself again."

"I did what I thought was right." I turned around to face the both of them. "If that makes me a bad man, then so be it."

Rika stood, a half-smile on her face. "You're not a bad man, Statford. Just an asshole. We'd have done the same thing."

"I wouldn't." Renton crossed his arms.

"Okay, most normal people would have done the same thing." Rika rolled her eyes at Renton, then back to me. "Harley sent up this report about the blood found at the animal hospital." She handed me the thin folder.

Reading it took about two minutes. "So there was a huge pool of the stuff there, and no body," I summarized. "Tracks were found leading away from the site to where a large car or van was possibly parked." I looked up at Rika. "I was right. There was more than just the lone bomber."

"That is the only thing keeping you from being behind bars tonight, Tommy." Rika held out her hand for the report, which I returned. "Whoever died there had friends who likely watched him do it. These are some sick people." Her desk phone, hidden under at least three inches of paperwork, rang. She snaked her hand through the layers of bureaucracy and found the handset. "Elder." She listened for a moment. "Okay. I'll be right down." She hung up and looked at Renton. "We might have something. Keep an eye on him."

"At least one," Renton agreed. "Both when I can manage it."

"Okay. I'll be right back." Rika walked to the door, looked over her shoulder, then opened it and left.

I watched Renton as she left. His eyes, even hidden by the sunglasses in the dim light, were tracking her every movement. It was only as she shut the door that his head almost imperceptibly moved in my direction. I crossed my arms over my chest and pinched the bridge of my nose, another headache threatening.

"Are you all right, Tom?" He sounded genuinely concerned.

I took a deep breath and blew it out. Looking at Renton, I said, "Dude, really? You and her! Really?" I laughed in little more than self-defense.

A very slight smile formed on his face. "She is a remarkable woman."

"Just what I needed in my head; I hope you two are happy." I made a beeline for the door.

I had gotten maybe three steps when an iron hand clamped on my left bicep. "Where do you think you're going?"

"Two things: lunch and a new phone. I'm still incommunicado with anyone, and I haven't eaten in a very long time."

"Wait until Rika gets back. We'll go together."

"I don't need a babysitter, man." I tried pulling my arm away with no success. "I just need a couple of tacos and a new phone. I think I can handle that without killing anyone."

Renton was unmoved. "We will go together, Tom."

"Fine." I put all the disgust I could into the word as I found a chair. I checked the calendar. Remarkably, it was still just the nineteenth. Six days until Christmas and I had probably scarred my niece and nephew for life, along with my sister disowning me, and when my mom got back, her killing me for breaking down her door. Add to that my wife was with her parents a thousand miles away while a friend and my mom's protégé found "twue wust", and it made for a very unhappy holiday.

Bah humbug.

Chapter Eight

It was with a decidedly not-merry attitude that I accompanied Renton and Elder to Rey Tolteca, a Mexican place I normally ate with Susana. If Rika and Renton noticed my lack of enthusiasm, they didn't seem to show it, or to care at all. Whether this was on purpose or they were truly oblivious, I couldn't say. Regardless, I knew I was going to have a less-than-stellar time.

What irked me most was just the idea that they thought I need babysitting. After all, it wasn't like my car was blown up, or my sister disowned me for busting into the house like I was a godsdamned action hero, or I had given my niece and nephew PTSD, or scared the shit out of some poor teenager, or seen some guy cut out his own frigging heart while smiling some creepy grin. I mean, it isn't like anything really bad had happened to me, right?

I hated the way my brain seemed to be whining about all that happened. I'm not normally so morose, but when I start getting kicked down, over and over again, I begin to take it personally. Keeping a stiff upper lip is all well and good, but if I didn't vent, I was likely to punch out the next person who asked me how I was. If it was whining, then so be it. Most people complain that they had to stay at work an extra half an hour. Others moaned they had gotten rice instead of beans with their entrees, and that was the end of the world for them. I've been present at the possible end of the world several times; I think I have a bit of room to bitch.

It was about half-past one in the afternoon when we arrived at the restaurant, and even with the cold weather and the time, the place was pretty busy. Luckily, I knew the owner of the place and had helped him through a tight spot. It was a mundane tight spot, not involving gods, demons, devils, mythological creatures or monsters from another plane of reality. It truly was a breath of fresh air, and proved to me that I could make a living as a regular private investigator, and I had no need for the Conclave. They might have needed me, but I had no need for them. As a result of having an in, we got a booth with barely any wait.

Elder and Renton took one side of the booth while I took the other. One of the waitresses, Millie, dropped off fresh tortilla chips and salsa, then took our drink orders, her English unaccented since she was a third-generation American. I pretty much lost my appetite the moment I realized our destination. I would have settled for a run for the border; coming to Tolteca without Susana seemed like cheating. I would have been content with not uttering a single word besides my order, but it seemed both Rika and her new paramour were of a different mind.

"So what was the feather, Tommy?" Rika dipped a chip into salsa and popped it in her mouth.

I said nothing as I reached for a chip of my own.

Renton smacked my hand as if I were a wayward child. "The lady asked you a question, Tom." The bastard then took the chip I wanted and popped it into his mouth. "There's no need to be rude."

My eyes rolled so hard I thought they'd fall out of my head and bounce on the table like marbles. "It's nothing. Just from a bird."

"What bird?" Renton pulled the bowl of chips towards him and Elder.

"Something called a quetzal. Who cares?" I took a drink of my soda, the caffeine breathing a bit of new life into me.

Rika chided me. "You certainly did when you went off to find out what it was."

"Doesn't matter much now, does it?" I snapped. "I have you two lovebirds chained to my hip until who fucking knows, and you want to question my godsdamned judgment every step of the way. So I ask again: who fucking cares?"

"Now, Tom," Renton began, "We're only trying to help you." He put a restraining hand on Rika's arm, which had started to vibrate with barely-contained rage.

"Help me, huh?" I reached over and took the bowl of chips out of his grasp. A few spilled to the table. "Help isn't exactly what I need right now." I bit into a chip, the crunching blotting out the rest of the world, if only for a moment. "I need someone to stop treating me like I'm a godsdamned lunatic for five fucking minutes, and having you two as babysitters isn't fucking helping." I hissed, "Now, can I just be allowed to think for a minute before I start telling you two shit that might not make a lick of sense? Do I have your permission for that, or do I need a note from my mom?" I sneered.

Rika exploded. "Fuck you, Statford!" She was so angry she sputtered the first word. Though she didn't shout the words, they were so clear, clean and concise the conversation in the immediate vicinity cut off instantly. "We are trying to back you up. I'm trying to back you up. The only reason your selfish ass is not on lock down is because of my fucking say-so. I could have you in jail for the next six thousand years if I wanted!" She pulled her arm away from Renton and pointed at me with a jabbing finger. "I stick my neck out for you because you're a friend, and you're in a bind. Don't you think for one second I will hesitate to knock you on your ass if you keep this shit up. Try me!"

Gods help me, I almost bit back at her. My shoulders tensed, the first bit of adrenaline went into my system, and I was just about ready to fight. It was a natural reaction to everything that happened so far. I was pretty much on the run, off-balance on my home turf, and seemingly a constant one step behind these bastards who were looking more like mental ghosts than anything else. If it had been anyone else, they would have been locked up or just mercifully shot on sight. Yet they still believed in me, and still wanted to help me.

I took a deep breath and let it out slowly, trying to get my cool back. She had called it exactly what it was: my selfishness. "Okay, Rika, you're right."

"Damn right I am." Her eyes bored into mine.

"And I'm sorry."

"Damn right you are." Her lips formed a small smile.

I chuckled. "Don't push your luck." That got a larger smile from Rika and a small laugh from Renton. "Okay, so we have a feather from a quetzal bird, a guy cutting his own heart out who also knows explosives, and no motive."

"Let's not forget his partners," Renton said. "He certainly didn't drag his own corpse away."

"Fair point. I haven't seen many things cut out parts of themselves and walk away. At least not this week," I amended. As I reached for a chip, my dinner companions looked at me wryly. I took a glance to my left and saw Millie, looking a bit green from the conversation.

"Oh." I was sheepish. "Sorry. I'll have the combo number twenty." I smiled as innocently as I could as Rika and Renton gave their orders. After Millie hurried away, I shook my head. "I'm not usually that careless."

"About?" Rika asked.

"Talking about the weirdness in public." I unrolled my silverware from the napkin; Rey Tolteca was famous for having meals out almost as fast as they were ordered. "I haven't talked about it in a long time."

"You mean like the events in New Orleans, Tom?" Renton nodded. "I can understand why you don't, especially as you chose to leave that life."

"It would be nice if the life left me. Did you know that yesterday a Greek god wanted me to find something for him?" Both shook their heads. "Seriously. Six months, six visits from different gods, and after New Orleans, Zeus thinks I'm just going to drop what I'm doing, the week before Christmas, no less, and find a set of cufflinks that he left somewhere."

"Cufflinks? Don't they wear togas?" While worldly, Renton was not as clued-in on the weirdness as other members of my family.

"Nope. They've kept with the fashions of the times." I took a drink of soda. "It was just a way to get me back in the game. I've been doing okay as a regular investigator, so they must have thought all was forgiven and enough time had passed for my tiny mortal mind to get over it." I laughed bitterly. "I will never 'get over it.'"

The food came, smelling so much like heaven I thought I had died and gone there. One thing I could say about Rey Tolteca: the portions were never skimpy, even for their combination platters. We ate in silence for a few minutes, savoring the beef, the chicken, the vegetables. As I ate, I kept going over what I said in my head. I really wanted absolutely nothing to do with the Conclave anymore. I was happier without them in my life, and I didn't need them anymore, if I ever did. It was a liberating feeling.

"Tom, your mother told me of your…" he paused before finding the right word, "duties. Why do these beings keep bothering you when you say you've so vehemently quit?"

I put down my fork and thought of a good analogy. "You ever have a dog?" Renton nodded. "You get a dog, and you have to train him to do things, like go outside to take care of business, get the paper, sit, beg, all of those neat little tricks. These are things you have to do, right?"

"Yes, but I don't see the point."

"Well, you have this dog," I continued, "and he's been a good boy. Does all the tricks and a few you didn't teach him. Loyal and good and everything a dog should be. All is right in the world with you and your dog." I picked up my fork again and cut a piece of an enchilada. "One day, though, your dog saves you from a burning building. He sits and looks like he wants an extra treat for doing so. You give him the treat and throw another one into another building. Then you set that building on fire with a flamethrower." I popped the enchilada in my mouth, chewing thoughtfully. "When the dog comes out of the flames, smoking and singed, is it any wonder he snaps at you?"

Rika nodded. "That doesn't answer his question."

I continued. "So Animal Services comes to take your dog away from your cruel and crazy ass. You totally flip out and scream that it's your dog, and you fight to keep him. Why fight to keep him? Because he's your property, and you can do what the fuck you want with him." I pointed the fork at my chest. "Woof woof."

Renton offered a commiserating smile. "I'm sorry. I didn't mean to pry."

"Sure you did," I countered. "You're a spy. It's your job. No harm, no foul, though." I devoured the last of my enchilada and went to work on my quesadilla. "I can't really blame them for thinking like that, though. They see us as pets, and like any pet, some are wild, some are tame. Some are usable. It sucks, but they're gods and we aren't. They have the power, and we have to just deal with it."

Another silence fell, this one a bit more companionable. I rarely talked to people about the why of the weirdness, as most just wanted to know what each particular god was like. I'm not much of a press agent; very few of them got more than a grunt and a terse description from me. For the ones I wasn't on a first name basis with, I usually had to depend on Larry for information.

Speaking of which, I whispered Larry's name to summon him. When he appeared, I muttered for him to do a quick once-around the restaurant. I made the mistake of not minding my surroundings before; that would not happen again.

No sooner had I done so than he reappeared at my side, his eyes wide. "Thomas! The front door!"

I swung my eyes around casually and there he was. It wasn't the same guy, I was sure of it. The face was different and this one was taller, but the features were highly similar, and the guy was wearing a tuxedo. I couldn't understand the significance of the tux; all I knew was this made proof positive that I was dealing with a group of wackos and not just some lone nut.

My eyes kept going in a path that would keep me from looking directly at him. "Throw money down. We're going." I shrugged my shoulders to give myself better access to my gun. With the guy in my peripheral vision, I saw he was just standing and watching me, as if waiting for me.

Rika looked up from her gigantic burrito. "Why?"

"There's another one here," Renton guessed, and smiled grimly "Front door?" I nodded. "Good." He threw down several twenty dollar bills. "How do you want to play this?"

"The Ray Stantz method," I smiled. Rika looked at me confused, but Renton seemed to get the reference.

"Subtle." Moving his chair back, he got up, subtly pulling Rika with him. "Follow me. Around the way to the back." They left, Rika not understanding what was going on.

Counting to five, I turned my gaze to my stalker and tipped my finger in salute. Instead of frustration or anything I would expect, a wide toothy grin broke out on his face. I got up quickly and made for the door. He waved at me with what seemed to be practiced nonchalance, turned and walked quickly out the door.

"Oh bullshit you think you're getting away," I growled as I pushed my way through the seeming wall of people, finding spaces to slip through. Some folks got pushed a little harder than they thought they deserved, but at that point, their comfort wasn't my concern. With a grunt after being crushed between two people who could make up five, I managed to slam myself against the door and push out into the biting mid-afternoon air.

The cold shocked me, the wind burning down my lungs and slapping me in the face, bringing my senses completely up on alert. I raked my eyes across the parking lot while heading for the cars. Rey Tolteca sat about two hundred feet from where all the cars parked, and there weren't all that many. I was rather glad for that as I saw the bastard walking across the snow and ice without a care in the world. He was about a hundred yards from me and getting farther with every step.

I kept my feet as I made my way across the road in front of the restaurant to the lot. While I wasn't slipping and sliding like at the hospital, I would never be mistaken for a winter athlete. He seemed to be heading for a corner of the lot that was completely empty, which was odd, and he was slowing down, which made even less sense.

Because there were not many cars in that part of the lot, the snow that fell and was still falling gave me a bit more traction. The deep drifts were a bitch to pull my feet out, but having the extra stability was an excellent trade. I knew I looked insane, my coat flying behind me as I hop-ran through the snow after a guy in a tux. It sounded like a really involved joke, but the laughing was nowhere near the surface for me.

Hearing crunching from behind me, I chanced a glance over my shoulder. Running like determined death was Renton, covering the same ground in a hell of a lot less time. Rika brought up the rear, speaking rapidly into her cell phone.

I turned around to see the guy just stopped only fifty feet ahead, then turned to face me. I hit the brakes and pulled my weapon. The chill wind tore at my bare right hand, making me grit my teeth in pain. The barrel never wavered from his chest; my mind closed off sensation to my hand and the pain eased. I started walking closer.

"Who the hell are you people?" I shouted. Renton took up position to my left and slightly behind, his own gun out. "What do you want with me?"

The man gave no response other than a pleasant smile. It was disturbingly like the one on the guy I saw not a few hours ago: empty, like the smile of a trauma victim too hopped up on morphine and endorphins to realize just how badly he's hurt. There was no hate or anger or happiness in that grin. It was just an expression for his mouth to use while he didn't talk. There was little more than madness in his eyes, and it already devoured his mind. I watched the smile fade slightly as he began to talk.

"Larry!" I shouted. "Get in close to hear what he says."

The spirit materialized next to the man, less than an arm's length separating the two. Larry seemed to be listening intently as I kept approaching the nutcase. The wind blew his words to me, which I was clueless to understand. It sounded like the same dialect the first one used, which only cemented they likely knew each other and were from the same coven or cult or whatever the hell it was people called a gang of psychotic Mexicans in tuxedos.

"Hands above your head, pal!" I stopped twenty feet away with Renton flanking me. "I won't warn you again."

"Something isn't right here." Renton took two steps forward, his gun held in two hands. We watched the man raised his arms above his head, fists clenched.

I took a look at the guy, a very hard look. Tuxedo, beatific smile, closed eyes. He was acting just like the other guy with one difference: no knife. There he was, acting as if his life was about to end and there was no way he was going to be able to do it, unless he had an invisible knife in his hand, which he didn't. It just looked like a plastic handle with a wire coming out of it.

Oh fuck me.

"Get down!" Renton screamed as he spun around. I saw him leap for me. I saw the anger in his face at getting suckered. I saw the irrational hope that he was wrong.

When the world blew up behind him, I knew he wasn't.

The explosion was not as severe as the one in my office parking lot, but it was enough. My ears registered the thunderclap an instant after I saw the detonation. The pressure wave sent Renton flying into me, his shoulder cracking into my still-sore ribs. Air flew out of me in a rush as, for the second time in as many days, my body left the ground. This time I was being propelled by two hundred pounds of explosive-aided human being. I wasn't able to get out from under Renton before we hit the ground, which made it hurt so very much worse. My breath was knocked from me again, an exhalation that came out in a scream of equal parts anger and fear. I could feel Renton on top of me, unmoving, likely stunned by the blast. The ribs that screamed from the pressure on them thankfully were not broken, though it took just about everything I had to pull in a hitching breath. The air bit into my lungs, and I welcomed the pain; it meant I was still alive.

I patted Renton on the shoulder as a signal that I was okay; neither of us would likely be able to hear anything without it being shouted through a megaphone. When he barely moved, I half-screamed if he was all right. When he shook his head, I felt droplets on my cheek. When I looked at his face and saw the crimson bubble forming on his lips, I shouted for Rika to call an ambulance.

Sliding from beneath Renton hurt my re-damaged ribs badly, but I managed it. I kept him on his stomach and tried not to let him fall too far. The three or four inches he slipped to the cold, snow-covered ground were as steady as I could make them. I saw what was lodged in his back: a silver belt buckle, or what had once been part of one. The force of the explosion bent and twisted the metal into a barb, sinking in far enough to pierce his lung and with enough velocity to puncture ribs. Blood wheezed around the wound and dripped from Renton's mouth.

I pulled my jacket open and ripped off my shirt to cover the wound, all the while yelling for Rika to get an ambulance and some petroleum jelly for me. Blood seeped through the cloth onto my hands, but I kept steady pressure on the area around the metal. I knew with some petroleum jelly I could seal the wound enough to keep air from escaping, but that would be useless unless Renton got to a hospital.

"Stay with me, you sonofabitch," I muttered, barely hearing myself. "Don't you fucking die on me."

Renton shook his head slightly and mouthed the words "She'd be pissed." The blood bubble popped and reformed with the three mouth movements.

For a wonder, I laughed. I couldn't tell which "she" he was talking about, and for the moment, I didn't care. The tough bastard would pull through. He had to pull through.

I don't know how long I was there keeping pressure, but I was pushed to the side by emergency services. I scooted back on my ass and sat there, staying out of the way. I had done what little I could, and I hoped I had remembered the right first aid training. From what I saw, the EMTs were doing what I did, just a lot more efficiently and professionally. I breathed a small sigh of relief.

The bastards had made it personal. Renton was my mom's protégé, which made him as close to family as my sister. I glanced over at Rika, who was stone-faced, even though I saw the anger in her eyes. There would be a reckoning.

While they wheeled Renton into the ambulance and Rika rode in back, I trudged back to my Toyota. I would meet them at the hospital and figure out what to do next. These goons were about to learn a prime lesson.

Nobody fucks with my family.

Chapter Nine

One of the most powerful senses is not sight, which can be fooled with something as simple as a switch of perspective. Hearing is right out, too, as few could tell the difference between live or Memorex, or tricks of echoes. Touch and taste? Sometimes they helped in identifying things, but who would want to touch or lick everything, especially in this day and age? I don't like to get that close to many people anyway. What was left?

The sense of smell can take you anywhere and anytime. Getting a whiff of baking bread or cookies can take you back to childhood. The scent of a particular perfume can send your mind back to your first real date, the one where you were able to drive yourself and your girl to the local burger joint and try and fail to be suave and debonair. Smell can take you so many great places.

Of course, it can also bring back memories you wish would stay buried. The reek of decomposing bodies in a swamp, left over from a lunatic voodoo priest. The cooking pork scent of burning flesh rising from the charred remains of a human being. The rank stench of corruption and madness, so thick it chokes you into sickness and disgust. It fills you with the desire to run away in fear. It doesn't matter where you run, just as long as you run far and fast and you don't stop. It goes back to the early days of humanity, when we would catch whiffs of predators stalking us and fires racing after us, and it gave us a chance to get away, to live, to survive.

Not everything is so dramatic, though. Sometimes, a scent will just remind you of a place you hated. The smell of antiseptic warring with sickness, pungent in the air. It coated my throat with a slick film I despised and would spend hours trying to push to the back of my mind. I knew it was in my head; this was not the first time I had been in a hospital over the years, and likely wouldn't be the last time.

It was the first time, however, I had been in hospital watching a machine breathe for a friend.

I had stuck around the crime scene for a few minutes giving my statement. I left out any of the weirdness to better make my way to the hospital, but it was still an hour before they let me leave, and that was only because they would drive me there. Something about my having problems following speed limits and traffic laws. Imagine that.

I had met Rika in the waiting room, where hope and despair were constantly locked in a never-ending battle. She sat in one of the usually uncomfortable chairs, leaning forward, her right leg bouncing. I had known her long enough to realize just how angry she was by the speed her leg bounced up and down. She had that coiled energy, wound tight as a spring, the kind that would explode the moment one thing, just one godsdamned thing more, happened. I had no desire to be that trigger.

Rika sprang up to meet me, and before I could hold up my arms in any kind of defense, she had already latched on. I felt her arms around me, her heart hammering through her chest onto mine. My breath was squeezed out of me, but I did not pull away. To do so would have been callous and cruel, and she was one of the few friends I had left. I couldn't do that to her; I wouldn't do that to her.

I put my own arms around her to comfort her. "It's going to be okay, Rika," I soothed without trying to sound like an idiot.

"He's been in surgery since he got here," she said, tears close but not daring to fall. "The doctor said he was in no real danger, even though the damage was pretty bad."

"How bad is pretty bad?"

"That piece of metal broke through a rib," she reported, pushing away from me and holding herself. Her head was down as she recited what she was told with mechanical accuracy. "It came up in an angle, going in a diagonal into his lung." Rika hiccupped a sob away before continuing. "They're saying what you did kept him from bleeding out or into his lung. Thank you."

I tried a smile on. "Glad I was of some use. He'll be okay. My mom wouldn't have taken him on if he wasn't tough enough to handle a collapsed lung."

That brought a snort of laughter from her. "She does know how to pick them." Rika sat down again, leaning forward as before but not bouncing her leg. "The doctor said it's a fairly straight-forward repair, but not something he'll be able to walk off in a few days."

Sitting down next to her on her right, I felt the tension still surrounding her. It was more muted than it was, but it was still there. "I wish I could take it back, Rika. I really do."

She gave me one of her patented looks that questioned my sanity. "What are you talking about?"

"I should have shot that guy. Kneecapped him, blown the detonator out of his hand, put two in the ten-ring, something." I sighed. "This is my fault."

The blow to the back of my head was physical this time, knocking me forward. I looked over to see Rika drawing back to hit me again. "Knock that shit off, Statford. This wasn't your fault."

"How do you figure? I didn't do anything to stop it."

"You couldn't have known. You were expecting a knife this time and why shouldn't you?" She hit me again, this time in the shoulder. "You aren't God. You can't know everything."

"No, but I can tell you I'm not much for letting someone get hurt in my place."

"That happens, and it's not your fault." Rika gently put her hand on my shoulder where she had hit it. "You're going to have to wake up and realize you aren't going to be prepared for everything. You aren't a Boy Scout." She laughed almost silently. "You aren't even a cub scout. You're a human being, no better and no worse than any other human being.

I leaned back in the truly uncomfortable chair, my mind heavy. Scrubbing my face roughly with my hands brought spots to my eyes. "So what do you want me to do, Rika? You want me to just not worry for those I care about? You want me to just not bother anymore with trying to keep people alive?" I laughed humorlessly. "That's why I got out of the game in the first place. I got tired of having to worry about protecting me and mine while prancing about to the tune of a bunch of immature children who rule reality according to their own whim. I couldn't do it anymore." I took a deep breath and said, "The price if I ever failed is too great."

We sat together in a companionable silence. I'm not much for self-analysis; I prefer analyzing others before getting into the labyrinth that is my own mind. Admittedly, I'm screwed up in the head. I would have to be to deal with even a fraction of the insanity I have seen over the years. That I hadn't eaten a bullet or took a dive off the Coleman Bridge meant I was made of stuff stronger than steel, or I was a stark raving lunatic. Neither sat well with me, but being able to handle the stresses the Conclave threw at me was a good thing in the grand scheme of things. Also, the likelihood of both things being true wasn't outside the realm of possibility.

The doctor finally came out, her face hidden behind a mask. Rika was up in an instant and I was right behind her. The doctor pulled down her mask, a thin smile behind it. "He's going to be fine."

I let out a long breath of air. At least he didn't die because of me. "How bad is it?"

"He won't be singing or dancing anytime soon, and considering this is probably the fourth time that lung as collapsed in his lifetime, he got off lucky." The doctor looked tired, with her eyes having more luggage than Samsonite underneath them. "He has more scar tissue than any human being I've ever seen, but he'll live."

"Can I see him?" Rika was nearly vibrating.

"We've got him pretty doped up, but yes." She looked at me. "I take it you're the Tom Statford he was asking about?" I nodded. "Good. The both of you can go in at the same time. Less hassle that way, and you can both leave at the same time."

Rika flashed her badge. "He's under protective custody at this time, Doctor. He's a witness in a possible attempted double homicide. I'd rather keep an eye on him myself."

I had never heard Rika pull her badge out for something like this; usually she assigned a couple of uniformed officers for the detail. Then again, he was kind of special to her. I did the same thing when Susana and I were in hospital together, so I couldn't begrudge her being his guardian angel. I did the smart thing and kept my mouth shut.

The doctor seemed too tired to care and beckoned us to follow her. With the scent of antiseptic all over the place, I couldn't get away from it. Our shoes made small squeaking noises on the floor as we made our way down the hall. We passed two rooms I knew quite well from personal experience before making it to room 316.

"Visiting hours will be over soon," the doctor said. "She can stay, but you will have to leave, sir."

"I understand, Doc. I'll be gone soon." I pushed the door open to enter the room, Rika on my heels.

Mister Renton lay in bed on his left side, a tube sticking out of the hole in his back. The piece of metal that struck him from explosive force was in an evidence bag, likely well on its way to Harley Blackwater along with my torn shirt and whatever was left of the bomber. Renton looked a bit pale but otherwise still imposing, even if he was wearing only a hospital gown and what looked to be enough wires stuck to him to do lights and sound for a rock concert. The eyes were bright and alert as he watched us enter. Rika dragged a chair over in front of him and sat, her hand taking his. I could see the firm squeeze he gave, and the smile she got on her face from his reaction.

"I won't ask how you are, Mister Renton," I said, trying to break the ice.

"With the amount of painkillers going through my system right now, I might actually tell you." Renton smiled tightly.

I started to apologize. "Renton, look, I---"

"Tom, if you apologize, I will get out of this bed and hurt you," he paused for breath, "rather badly. I will then be forced to stay in hospital for quite a bit longer." There was another pause, then, "I would rather not have either of those conditions occur."

"I tried explaining it to him," Rika said. "He might understand now that you put it so well."

"Doubtful." A quick breath, then, "I know his mother."

"Fair enough, Renton," I said. "You know I'm going after them, right?"

He nodded. "It's what I would do."

"You mean *we're* going after them," Rika interjected.

Renton and I spoke in unison. "No!"

Within a blink, Rika was in my face. I saw the anger and hurt in her eyes; she was ready to get those bastards. "What the hell do you mean no? I am in this as much as you are and you know it. Look Statford, you cannot do this alone! I barely parted my lips to speak, when she gave me the hand.

'Rika," the sound of Renton's course, raspy voice struck a nerve. I swear I could see the hair on the back of her neck stand straight up. She whipped around sharply to Renton.

"And you Mister don't make me call you by your full name Renton, you could have died! Hell, how many times does one have to collapse the same lung?

"Rika, I jus…"

"I don't give just a damn what you want!" She plopped down in the chair, frustrated arms crossed like a child who couldn't get her way. "I will be damned if I just sit her and wait for those fuckers to strike again."

I held up a hand to stop both of them from talking. "Look, that's all well and good you want to go after them, but I need you here. I don't know if he's going to be okay for sure, and I don't know if these guys will come along and try to finish the job."

"They won't, though," Rika countered. "They aren't after him. They're after you."

"Tom doesn't know that," Renton wheezed. "Neither do you."

I put my hand on her shoulder. "Don't worry, Rika. I will find them." I gave her shoulder a squeeze to reassure her. "I will find them and I will make sure they don't do anything like this ever again."

"Good hunting, Tom," Renton said, his voice somewhat stronger.

I nodded my head to him and left, my coat flowing behind me. Slowing down my pace let the coat fall to my legs so I didn't look like the Angel of Death stalking the halls of a hospital. I shoved my hands into my pockets and tried to bring all the elements together.

So far, I had two corpses, both dead by their own hand. There was the blown-up car, the feather, the stone knife. There was the prayer the two dead guys spoke before they decided to punch their own tickets, a prayer in a language that, according to Larry, only a million people in the entire world spoke. There was the way they seemed to want to keep me guessing, keep me wondering what the hell they were doing. None of it made any sense, though.

Were they trying to intimidate me? If so, they were failing miserably. If anything, I wanted to find them and let them know my displeasure at their actions more than ever. I would show exactly how pissed I was and just how unafraid I was of them. If anything, their actions struck me as bumbling, almost comical. I would have laughed if Renton didn't have a tube in his back; that took the mirth right out of it.

If they actually were trying to kill me, they were quite possibly the most inept assassins on the face of the earth. The two I had met showed no professionalism, no real regard for their target. Even if I'm not some president or potentate, I was still someone rather important, and I knew enough to keep myself safe from damned near anything. The closest they had gotten was in the beginning of this fiasco, and even then it was obvious they had no real desire to kill me.

That left me with a big fat bupkis as far as motive. In every crime, there is always that big question: *cuo buono*. Who benefits? It's what cops call motive, and it fits right in with means and opportunity. It is that thing that answers that big question. Why? You could usually break the motive down to one of four things: love, ego, money, or revenge. Sometimes it ended up being more than one, but for the most part, it was only one motive at heart. None of the situations struck me as any of those reasons. It wasn't love, unless I had some fanatical groupies who couldn't handle I was married. Money? Sure, I had some after investing wisely following a pair of high-paying cases, but I was no threat to anyone in the financial field. Ego made no sense, either. I didn't usually deal with the Lex Luthor supervillain types of bad guys; I dealt with more the common everyday bad guy. Granted, they usually had supernatural tendencies, but nothing too out of this world.

That left revenge, and even that made absolutely no sense whatsoever. I had no clue who these assholes were. What little I knew didn't put them anywhere near Conclave territory, so I couldn't have pissed off any of the usual suspects who might use mortal agents to go after me. That was kind of the loophole in the protection I was gifted by being the Keeper: a god couldn't smite me, but hired hands could make my life miserable, short, or both. This didn't have the feel of a hit, though, and I knew how hits felt.

So there I was, standing outside the Hampton Care Center Plex in the middle of December, snow and ice falling from the dark sky, and I had absolutely no clues. I had no leads. I wasn't even sure if I wasn't just imagining some grand conspiracy against me, and that it wasn't just some fruitcakes with a penchant for tuxedos trying to make my life a living hell. In total, all I possessed was nothing, at least as far as figuring out what the living hell was going on. A case with no clues wasn't a case. I leaned against a convenient pillar and pondered the twilight sky.

It was just a good way to drive yourself crazy.

"Tommy?"

Rika's voice came from behind me. I turned my head and looked at her. I beckoned her over with my head, keeping my hands warm in my pockets. "What's going on?"

She came at me with both barrels. "You think I don't know why you don't want me along for this?"

I turned the rest of my body and put my back to the pillar. "No, I know you know why," I countered. "You're not stupid. I know this. I also know that someone needs to keep an eye on him."

"Renton can handle himself. Besides, he's in bed. He's not going anywhere."

"Wrong, Rika. I know him. I know what my mom said to him. He's likely devising a scheme to get discharged so he can come along with this hunt, punctured lung and all."

Rika's dark skin went ashen. "He wouldn't dare."

"You've met my mom, right?" When Rika nodded, I continued. "You know the kind of loyalty she inspires. Without a doubt, Renton would throw himself into a wood chipper for her."

"So when you say you want me to keep an eye on him, you mean you want me to make sure he doesn't do anything stupid."

"Pretty much."

Rika bit her bottom lip with a sigh. "Okay. I can do that."

"Good. I know how you two feel about each other." A rush of color came back to her face and her cheeks began to beam as she looked down at the ground. "And I don't really care what it takes. He needs to stay immobile so he can heal. You can do that, and I know you will do what it takes to keep him that way, by any means necessary. I'll handle the nutballs."

"How did you know? About us, I mean."

"I'm smarter than I look, Elder," I smirked, "and the way he couldn't keep his eyes off of you whenever you moved, was also a dead giveaway."

"Yeah, right, Statford! Besides, you're the one who walked outside without a way to get anywhere."

Dammit, I hated when she had a point. "Very true. I need a car."

"If you can wait a bit, I can get Susana's car out of impound and over here for you. It shouldn't take long, and I can make sure you get it as long as you don't go the TJ Hooker route again."

I laughed. Damn, it felt good to laugh in the cold and the dark; it dispelled some of the gloom. "I'll drive like Columbo, I promise."

She shook her head at me and pulled out her cell. After a few minutes and some terse words, she said, "Okay, it'll be here probably in the next thirty minutes. Remember, Statford: Columbo, not Hooker."

I held up my hands in surrender. "I promise, on my word of honor."

"Good. I'm gonna go back to our little patient and make sure he is resting like he is supposed to. "

As she turned to go, I called after her. "Wait a minute. I just have one more question."

She turned back to me, her hands shoved in her pocket, her eyebrow raised. Snow landed on her at a slant. "What is it, Tommy?"

I made my voice gravelly and squinted one eye while hunching over. "I just have to know: What is Renton's first name?"

Rika fought back a laugh as she headed back inside. She whipped her head around and opened her mouth to say something, but thought better of it. Her coy and adorable smile lit up the night as she rolled her eyes. It was like a last light of hope for me and she walked in the hospital. There I was alone in the snow.

Well, godsdammit.

Chapter Ten

The wind made little twisters out of loose snow crystals. They danced across the top level of parking lot belonging to the Hilton in Virginia Beach. The sun had been down for hours, and the snow had been a steady companion for that time, hiding any trace of tire tracks or footprints exposed to the sky. All across the lot were large mounds of snow, each a car or truck or van covered in the stuff. For all anyone could see, they were forgotten in the cold, while their owners stayed in the warmth and the light.

Driving to Virginia Beach was an extreme exercise in patience, considering I made a stop before the hotel. I also got stuck behind two trucks along the way, each spreading salt in a seemingly futile attempt to keep the roads drivable. According to the local people who studied meteors, the front that brought all the white stuff falling was parked right on top of the Hampton Roads area, also covering the Eastern Shore to the north and the Outer Banks to the south. The snow fell all the way up past Williamsburg, nearly shutting down the whole area. I made sure I drove as I promised, mostly because I had no desire to try and zoom past the trucks plowing and laying down salt. No need to invite disaster when I was most likely heading into it on my own.

The stop had been necessary, both to fill up the gas tank and to send a message. I was still incommunicado thanks to not having a chance to hit the cell phone store, so I resorted to more traditional methods of doing things. I made a mental note for the next time something happened to have a backup phone. I mean, I had a backup gun, so a backup phone would be useful. The broken one mocked me from its place on the floorboard, where I had thrown it just a scant half a day prior.

I felt things were happening just way too quickly. Two days ago, I was happy. Sure, I had to deal with the schmucks in the Conclave, but that was par for the course. Telling them to piss off was one of the pleasures in my life. In two days, I was nearly blown up twice, witnessed two suicides, nearly lost a friend to a metal spike in the lung, and convinced my sister I was a complete madman. That is usually enough for most people to consider a complete relocation to parts unknown, where no one can find them and let the world handle itself.

That would be the sane thing to do. Sitting there in Susana's Toyota, I was in nearly total darkness from the snow blanketing the windows. I was smart enough to bundle up for the weather and even brought some of those chemical hand warmers for the occasion. Most folks would be smarter and just start the car to access the heater, and admittedly I wanted to turn it on so I wasn't rubbing my hands and constantly thinking about the last scene in *The Shining*. I kept the car off so the snow would cover the car, giving me some manner of camouflage. Since the nutjobs liked getting close and personal, I figured I was pretty safe due to the snow. Even from their obvious non-reaction to the elements, they followed some laws of normal people, namely having to actually physically move from one place to another. They couldn't fly or teleport, which rather pleased me. It wouldn't have been the first time I dealt with things that flew or teleported, but thankfully it wasn't the case with these crazy bastards.

Every fifteen minutes or so, I would turn the car on for a moment to lower the windows an inch, knock away the snow, then raise them back up. It wasn't much of a viewport, but it gave me some idea of what was around me. Even if, from all indications, the crazies did not want to hurt or kill me, I didn't want to take the chance they would change their minds. I kept a watchful eye through the slits on both sides, and an ear open for anything that sounded like a lunatic with a stone knife or an explosive vest.

No, people like that don't have specific sounds, but only a really dedicated nutball would venture out into that weather just to kill someone they've failed to kill after two attempts.

I had just dropped the driver's side window when I heard a crunching on snow. I turned the car off and waited, my hand snaking into my coat to grip my gun and pull it out. My breath plumed in the cold on every exhale, and I tried to breathe shallowly so I would not make as much noise. I heard another crunch, this one more muffled and coming from possibly my left. That is one of the big problems with snow: you can rarely tell where a sound is coming from in it, as the white stuff drains the sound out of everything and confuses the direction where the sound originated.

When I heard a throat clear, I pulled the hammer back on my pistol. Even with the snow, it couldn't have been more than fifteen feet away. I unlocked the door and pulled the latch, readying to throw it open as best I could if the need arose. My gun was in my right hand, my finger just off the trigger. My reaction depended on the next few seconds.

I heard the throat clear again, this time only a few feet from the car. Then, in a playful tone, someone spoke.

"Allons-y!"

That cheeky son of a bitch.

I pushed the door fully open, struggling with the snow a bit but managing to get the opening wide enough for me to get out. My gun was still out but down at my side as my legs sank a full six inches into the snow. I scanned the area closely, making sure that the only people around were me and the newcomer.

He just stood there in front of the Toyota, seemingly impervious to the cold, though I'm sure the white cloak he wore insulated him from the weather. His hood was up, keeping the snow out of his face. He seemed to be standing on the snow rather than in it, as I could see the tops of his boots. It was an almost surreal thing, seeing him almost float on the surface of snow that had to be the better part of a foot deep. Of course, how could I expect Luc Bertrand, the head of the Assassin's Guild for the east coast to dirty his boots in common snow?

I put away my gun and trudged my way to him, my legs making a trail a bat could follow. I put out my hand as I approached, and he clasped my arm at the wrist, a symbol of friendship among the assassins. I had known Luc for several years, and whatever differences we had were ancient history. We respected one another in the ways of battle, and I owed him quite a bit. Granted, he owed me his life once or twice as well. However, once you get into mutual owing of lives, it kind of just settles into just one of those things that friends do for each other.

Luc swept back the hood of his cloak and smiled. He had let his hair grow quite a bit than when last I saw him, and he had a short ponytail of blond hair. His eyes, usually clear blue, had gone to green, though I couldn't be sure if it was natural or thanks to contact lenses. Luc was about as tall as me, but with a much more wiry build, the strength he had evident in his grip. The languid smile opened more, revealing perfectly straight white teeth. "I was wondering when you were going to break cover, Thomas." Luc's voice held the accent of his homeland of Tours, France. That he had not seen his place of birth in decades never seemed to bother him, though he often told me he wanted to go back.

"Better to be safe than sorry, Luc." I headed back to the car and got in, my finger hitting the unlocking button for the passenger side. "Hop in. I need to talk to you."

With a grace born from years of training and deadly practice, Luc strode carefully to the other side of the Toyota. It took him a few moments to get the door open, but he managed it. Once he was inside, I turned the engine over and hit both the heater and the defroster. Welcome blasts of warm air flowed from the vents, beginning the thawing of the windows and me. I let out a sigh of contentment.

"So your message indicated. You have been waiting for me long, Thomas?" Luc raised an eyebrow at me while removing his gloves.

"A little while," I admitted, holding my hands to the vent. "I couldn't be sure when you got the message." I hit the windshield wipers, forcing the snow off the glass and letting a view of Pembroke Town Center through.

"*Mon frère*, I came as soon as I was told. You are a good friend, and your message sounded most dire." The cloak opened, showing a black skintight outfit of some kind. Luc touched a small button on the collar of the suit.

I couldn't help myself. "What the hell is that?"

"Ah, a beauty, is it not?" Luc beamed. "It is a skinsuit, something we use in our work." He unzipped the wrists of the outfit and showed a lattice of lines on the inside of the outfit. "It is an all-weather suit, allowing comfort in even the most terrible climates. It keeps me warm when it is cold, and cool when it is hot."

"Frank Herbert, eat your heart out," I muttered. When Luc gave me a quizzical look, I dismissed it with a wave of my hand. "I didn't call you here to discuss men's fashions, Luc."

"That much is certain, as you are still wearing two year old jeans," Luc said.

I sighed. "Everyone's a critic." I put the car in Drive and pulled out of the parking spot, which took a bit of rocking back and forth. While I was on my way to the exit ramp, I continued. "I take it you heard about what's going on in my neck of the woods."

"Only that your car is no longer, and you were detained by the police."

"That's it?" I was shocked. Luc was the premiere information broker of the east coast, and not knowing all that had happened was incredible. "You didn't hear about the exploding guy at a movie theater, or someone getting a metal spike in their lung because of it? You don't know that Susana is out of town?"

Luc took a moment before answering. Driving through the garage was easier since everything was covered. "I do not intrude on your life any more than you wish, Thomas. I do this out of respect and friendship to both you and Susana. It is not my place to watch over you both, as I think it would be somewhat of an insult to have someone spy upon me."

Nodding, I brought us out onto Virginia Beach Boulevard, the street unsurprisingly empty due to the weather and the late hour.

Thursday had just become Friday, and that meant no one would be out and about. I took the turn that would get Luc back to the Oceanfront via the secondary interstate. "I appreciate that, man, but someone is after me."

"Oh, that much is certain." When I glanced at Luc, he gave a Gallic shrug. "Explosions are usually a good indicator that things are amiss."

I rolled my eyes then began to fill the assassin in about the last forty-eight hours. "Anyway, I've had to deal with a guy cutting his own heart out and another guy blowing himself up. They're either the most inept assassins on earth, or there's a reason they're pulling this crap. I'm open to opinions."

Luc sat for a moment as I drove, the wipers doing their job as we crept along at a sedate thirty miles an hour. "Can you describe them?"

"Medium height," I began, slowing the car down to twenty. "Hispanic. They might come from way down south past Mexico. That feels right to me." I thought carefully before continuing. "They wear the same tuxedos, like stone knives and explosives. I don't know how many of them there are, but I'm willing to bet there's a bunch of them."

"Tuxedos? Interesting." Luc tapped his fingers on the dashboard. "Why do you think they are from so far south?"

"One of them left behind a feather from a quetzal bird. I did a little digging and found out the bird is from around the Yucatan Peninsula."

"Google is making you lazy, Thomas," Luc said reprovingly.

A small smile formed. "Not Google. An actual vet told me. I know how to do more than type, Frenchie."

The nickname had the desired effect, a chuckle from the Frenchman. "You are a brave and foolish man. No wonder we are friends."

"Does any of that help?"

"I have found targets with less."

"These aren't targets, Luc. They're mine. I need answers, not corpses."

Luc harrumphed. "You would be surprised what kind of information I can get from a body."

I shook my head, keeping my eyes on the road. "No, Luc, I need them alive. Something is very hinky about this whole thing."

"Hinky? What does that mean?"

"It means wrong. Something is very off, and I want to know what it is." My hands squeezed the wheel. "I need to know what is going on and why. Someone got hurt and even though I know it wasn't my fault, I feel like it is."

"So you have to find out how things are wrong and fix them in your completely misguided sense of honor." Luc tutted at me. "Thomas, your sense of duty is going to get you killed one day."

I nodded and smiled. "It won't be today."

The assassin laughed and zipped up the wrists of his suit. "You are a great man, Thomas Statford. No wonder the gods wish to be back in your good graces."

That brought my head around, even if only for a second. "What does that mean?"

"It is no secret that the gods are not pleased to have lost you. Insidia herself has approached me twice." He flapped his hand dismissively. "She tried to force me to, in her words, bring you to your senses." Insidia was the goddess of treacherous ambush, and essentially the goddess of assassins. I had gotten Luc to swear an oath by her, making sure that any contracts he took would be more than the wanton assassinations that the guild was known for undertaking. "I told her that I may be your friend, but I will not force you into anything. You are much too stubborn and hard-headed for that."

I was almost touched by Luc's sentiment. "What did she say?"

"She asked me to reconsider, before it was too late. Again, her words."

"Too late for what?" We arrived at the Oceanfront, the strip lit up with white, red, and green lights for the holidays. I took the left turn and slowly made my way to Luc's nightclub, the Umbra Motus.

"She refused to say, only that you were being an obstinate fool, and blaming them for something that they did not do."

"Bullshit they didn't do it!" The words escaped me before I could clamp down on my anger. "Sorry, Luc. I just get so agitated by their constant claims of innocence. It's damned tiresome."

"Of course it is, Thomas. Being betrayed is never something to be taken lightly, and you have that right. I am almost surprised you have not been more forceful with your refusals."

"There's only so much I can do to a god. They may not be able to hurt me directly, and I can't hurt them directly either. Sometimes, though, I wouldn't mind giving them some wall-to-wall counseling." When Luc said nothing, I looked at him quickly. From his expression, he didn't get the reference. "I mean grab them and throw them from one wall to another so their attitudes change."

Luc let out a snort of laughter. "You Americans and your sayings. So violent."

"This coming from an assassin?" I countered.

"You do have a point, though I do not kill mindlessly. I never stop the thoughts of another without reason, and I certainly do not enjoy it. Assassins have been a necessity of every society since time immemorial."

"I won't argue that." We pulled into the Umbra's empty lot, barely a dusting of snow on the blacktop. I could even see the yellow lines marking the spots. "Wow, what do you have under there? Some kind of heating element?"

"Oh, you mean the lot? I have my apprentices clean it."

At his words, five people came out of the club's front door, holding shovels in their hands. In only a few minutes the lot was clean. I mean it was completely clear of any snow, ice, or sludge. I wouldn't say you could eat off of it, but you definitely wouldn't have to worry about slipping and sliding on the way in or out of the lot.

"Wow," I said again. "You think you can help me find something out, Luc?"

Luc nodded, pushing the small button on his suit. "I may need some time, of course. Will you be able to hold off any crazed rampages through the area while driving at high speeds?"

My expression was one of exasperation. "I think I can, Frenchie."

"Ah good!" Luc pulled his gloves on and I noticed how well the material molded to his hands. I had to get me one of those suits. "I should have something for you by sundown. What you have given me is enough, I think. I will look into it personally."

"Thanks, Luc. I owe you," I said, holding out my hand.

"Nonsense!" Luc smiled as he grasped my wrist again. "We are friends, and friends do not owe one another." As he released me, he laughed again. "Perhaps one of these days you will wake up and realize that."

"One day, Frenchie. Not today."

"Of course." Luc pulled the hood of his cloak over his head. "I have business to attend elsewhere tomorrow, but I will send a trusted apprentice to you."

"You won't call?"

"I cannot, Thomas. Your mobile is still a bit worse for wear."

I kicked myself mentally for forgetting. "Right. Of course."

"I will have something for you, *mon frère*. I promise." He opened the door and stepped out, the wind pulling his cloak over his left shoulder. "Get some rest, though. You need it."

"I'm at Susana's, so you can send the message there."

"I know." At my mouth dropping open in surprise, Luc grinned. "Just because I don't keep my entire attention on you does not mean I do not know where you are, Thomas. *Au revoir*."

I sat in the Toyota for a few minutes, letting the heater run full blast to rid the car of the chill that entered while the door was open. I knew Luc was right, and I needed rest. My sleep had been ragged the night before, and I knew I was running on fumes. I also knew I wouldn't make it back to Susana's apartment until three in the morning. I cursed the weather and began the long drive back to the Peninsula. I hoped Luc would find something that would lead me to this group of fools who wanted to screw up my life.

By the time I got home, I was exhausted. All I had strength left to do was kick off my shoes, toss my coat to the floor, and fall into bed. I don't even think I felt my head hit the pillow. One thought followed me down into dreamland.

I hope this is all over soon.

Chapter Eleven

Racing down the hallway, my bare feet slapping flat against the tiles of the prison I called home, my heart pounding in my chest. Breath was heavy in my throat, a scream begging and pleading for me to release it into the cold still air. Tears ran down my face, stinging hot. I ran harder, trying to put as much distance as I could between me and the ones chasing me. I chanced a look behind me. The dim light came from overhead, little islands of luminescence marking the path I followed out of desperation. I heard growls from behind me, and a gross approximation of my name. There was a teeth-jarring crash as the door I had burst through only scant seconds ago flew open.

The monsters were getting closer.

I ran past door after identical blue door, numbers jumbled on the front of them, unidentifiable. Was it because of my tears or because of my head pounding? One of the ogres had hit me hard in the head, making me fall over and hurt my knees. The thin blue pants I wore were like pajama bottoms, light and airy. The right leg of them stuck to flesh thanks to my blood seeping from the banged-up knee.

Or was it my blood? I didn't know. The monsters had argued back and forth after the one hit me. I couldn't make out any words, but one was mad at the other for doing it. That was when I chose to run, and I ran as fast as I could. I knew there had to be some way out, some possible path to get rid of this horrible place where I was beaten and yelled at and called horrible things by those creatures.

Finally, I saw it.

A sign with red letters over the door, giving me hope, giving my feet speed. I moved faster than I had before. This wasn't the first time I had tried escaping this vile place, but it would be the last. I would be free. A smile formed on my chapped lips as my hand reached for the bar on the door.

It opened.

I sprang back, hissing and landing on my back. My feet and hands began to shove me away from the sight before me. Light poured through, eclipsed by a tall thin creature in white. In one hand it held a scroll, in the other a tiny stiletto. I feared the scroll more than the blade. I could dodge the blade, fight it, break it if I wanted. The scroll I could not fight because it was the Truth. I contained infinite knowledge about me, intimate details of all the things I had ever done. And it only said one thing, over and over, a mantra that pounded into my skull.

"It is all your fault."

The emaciated creature in front of me held up the scroll and began to chant. It rang through my ears, chilling me to the bone, freezing me to the core of my soul. I wept openly, my throat raw, my eyes burning, choked sounds coming from my dry chapped lips. I knew the chant, even though I had never heard it before. It was just two words; two words that chained me to the floor, turning my own body traitor against me.

Over and over, it chanted. I heard the two beasts that chased me down chanting as well. Again and again, the words were sing-song, all three in unison. I wanted to block my ears but my hands would not move. I wanted to scream and drown them out but my throat was locked; the best I could manage were thin whispering whimpers.

The gaunt figure raised the scroll. It dangled from its long fingers. The scroll was a pendulum, going back and forth. My eyes locked on to the vellum, seeing the nonsense scribbles that made one thing clear: that it was my fault, that everything was my fault that I must pay for my terrible crimes.

The creatures that chased me lifted me up, one arm apiece, and held me fast. They didn't need to worry; I wasn't going anywhere. When the gaunt giant before me raised the stiletto, the chant going to crescendo, I didn't fight it; I couldn't fight it. I just wanted it to be over.

With my chest bared, the giant plunged the stiletto down, screaming the words of the chant in near-orgasmic frenzy.

"It's time!"

I bolted upright in bed, sweat streaming from my pores. The wind outside had picked up something fierce, a mournful wail just beyond my window. It faded in and out rhythmically, just like the chant from my dream. My heart was tripping like a jackhammer. I laid back against the pillow, my breathing finally started to get back under control. Sympathetic tears fell, I squeezed my eyes tightly shut; I felt them roll down the sides of my face. "Another nightmare, Thomas?" Larry's voice came from the bedroom entrance. I nodded, not trusting myself to speak for the moment. "This could be an issue."

When I could talk, I asked, "Did I say anything?" My voice was raspy, as if my throat was dry like I had been running a marathon. "Anything at all?"

There was a pause, then Larry said, "It is not what you said. It is the crying, the clawing of the air as you sleep. Something preys upon you, Thomas; I do not like it. I almost thought you were not going to wake up."

I sat up, the blankets pooling on my lap. My hands rubbed my face hard, and I felt the stubble on my chin and jaw. "Is it anything unnatural? Are you, I don't know, sensing anything out there messing with my mind?" My question was one of pure speculation and desperation.

The spirit shook his head, certainty in the gesture. "You have not been tampered with, mind or body, Thomas, at least not that I have been able to detect."

"What about spiritually?" I swung my legs off the bed to sit more comfortably.

"You are possessed of one the most formidable wills I have ever met in my existence, Thomas. You would know." Larry glided over and stood across from me. "What was the dream?"

I told him, leaving out no detail. I mentioned the squeaking of the hinges, the scroll, the stiletto, and that gods-awful chant. Every possible thing I could remember, I told my friend. The drying sweat caused me a chill.

"You do not usually have these vivid of dreams, Thomas. This could be somewhat concerning." Larry was fast becoming the master of the understatement.

I pushed up quickly from the mattress, trying to get the nightmare out of my mind. I stripped off my clothes, which stuck to me from the fear-sweats. "It was so real, Larry. I mean it. I felt like I was actually there."

"Where?"

"I don't know." I sighed deeply as I walked to the shower. "It felt like a prison, but also like I had always been there. It was so bizarre." Stopping at the doorway, I looked back to Larry. "Like, I belonged there."

I took an extra-long shower, this time running out the hot water to try and scrub away the hellish dream. As I scrubbed the dried sweat from my body, my mind went over each factor of the dream, working to rationalize it away. I gave it up as futile after a few minutes; there was nothing to be done about it. It would go or it would stay. I had more important things to do.

Even though shaving would take only a few minutes, I skipped it. I was in a hurry and dressed in near-record time. I pulled on my shoes, took a deep and cleansing breath, and got ready to face the day. When I put on my coat, the leather a comfortable weight on my shoulders, I started feeling better. Evil-doers beware, and all that happy bullshit. Nothing would stop me from getting to the bottom of these well-dressed psychos. A confident smile bloomed on my face. This would be the day.

That determination died a swift and horrible death about three seconds later when I opened the apartment door.

The way our apartment building is set up is six units facing each other with three floors per building. They're all the rage in just about any low-rise complex, especially in Virginia. There were about five of them, all in a line, just down the Hampton Highway. They were a bit more expensive than most apartments, and I couldn't have afforded one on my own in addition to the rent for my office, but they were definitely worth the extra cash.

With the setup of the building, however, there was a problem in inclement weather, namely a wind tunnel effect that brought snow and ice and rain directly through, funneling it to almost gale-force at times. Just outside my door was a solid foot and some change of snow, and probably an inch or two of ice just beneath it. My across-the-way neighbors had it worse, as the wind had struck the breezeway just right and covered their door completely with a layer of snow.

I pulled my coat tight around me and trudged my way out of the apartment, trying to ignore the wetness seeping through my shoes and socks. Mostly, I was successful, though I knew this would not be the start of a good day by any measure. I kept hearing that voice in my head, the reasonable British one who liked to call me an idiot, tell me to go back inside and hibernate for the next couple of days. It was snowy and messy and all I'd likely accomplish is getting someone killed. I pushed the voice away firmly, letting it know in no uncertain terms that I was not going to be intimidated by nuts in tuxedos. It was also Christmastime, I told the voice. Susana needs to come home. The faster I finish, the faster she gets back.

When the voice had no reply for that, I smiled in spite of the biting bitter wind carrying the snow and ice on it. Sure, it was an empty victory, but at least I had something going for me. That warmed me up enough to get me through cleaning off the Toyota, which was completely buried under what felt like a ton of snow. By the time I got to where I was able to open the car door, I was exhausted, sweaty, and breathing heavily. Even though I was tempted to go back inside and climb back under the covers, I knew I had to get going. An earlier glance at the clock had the time around noon, and if anything, the Arctic trek and clean-off had taken at least thirty minutes. Sundown was no more than four or five hours away, which meant my time to get things settled and squared away before Luc showed up was limited.

As I sat in the car, the engine started, the heater blasting out blessed and welcomed hot air, I shook my head at my predicament. After so long of seeming to have all the time in the world, time was running out of it.

Moving out of the parking area and down the road at a sedate twenty miles an hour, I marveled at how everything seemed to be blanketed by winter. Even the roads, which had been salted and plowed almost religiously for the past several days, were completely covered, as if the entire Commonwealth of Virginia had decided to give up the fight against the elements. There was a desolation as far as I could see, with the way the tree limbs bent under the weight of the snow and ice, like they were trying to hold up the sky and failing. There were no other cars on the road, which surprised me. Virginia drivers will drive in the face of Armageddon, be terrible at it, and complain the whole time about the weather and other drivers. This time, though, I was the only fool driving.

The whisking of the windshield wipers was almost hypnotic, and I forced myself to focus on different things to keep from going to sleep. Even goosing the Toyota up to thirty didn't make me seem to go appreciably faster. As I took the turn to get to the nearest cell phone store, I came to a realization that should have been obvious from the time I stepped out the door.

Nothing was open.

I mean it, absolutely nothing. Even the grocery store near the place I got my phone and accessories, which usually had at least a skeleton crew at all times, was dark, the parking lot completely empty. No cars were in any of the spaces of the shopping center, the snow was pristine which meant no delivery trucks had gone around the back, and there weren't even any carts in the corrals. I stopped at the light, even though it was green, taking in the dark storefronts, the wind howling outside my car, blowing swirls of ice and snow into small twisters that fell apart almost the moment they were created. There was nothing out there for me.

Muttering a curse, I continued through the light, making my way back to the highway. For a gag, I turned the radio on. It had to be better than listening to the howling wail coming from outside.

"---indoors for the rest of the week," the radio blared, so loud I had to turn it down. "With the blizzard last night covering the entire Hampton Roads area in a foot of snow or more in some places, police and government officials are asking everyone to stay off the streets. Four deaths have been attributed to the storm, and with the way it's still coming down, that number is likely to rise, according to local authorities. VDOT has requested everyone who does not have a life-threatening emergency to stay off the road, as the plows have been unable to keep up with the snowfall." That was pretty serious. If the department of transportation was having trouble with the weather, I likely needed to get my ass back home. It wasn't like I could do much else.

With that in mind, I turned the radio off and made a beeline for the apartment. It was unlikely that I'd get anything done for the rest of the day, at least until the storm broke, and feeling like I was the last man on earth did nothing for my sense of well-being. I was disgusted that I had wasted an hour to make a ten-mile round trip. As I got out of the car and retraced my steps to the apartment door, the sounds of my steps were swallowed up by the snow.

It was powerfully lonely as I stood at the entrance to the apartment, my freezing fingers putting the key in the lock. I went inside, closed and locked the door, and stomped the snow off my feet, the clumps of white stuff falling away and melting quickly in the heated living room. I relaxed a bit, busying myself with puttering around the place, doing a couple of dishes, straightening things up, all that domestic stuff. When that took about ten minutes, I sat down and played some video games.

That lasted about five minutes before I tossed the controller down in disgust. Never before had I felt so restless and cut off from the world. I was sitting and waiting and trying to keep from going stir crazy. I was failing miserably, and I knew it.

"You are worse than a caged tiger, Thomas." Larry sat at the small dining table, legs crossed, resplendent in a form-fitting royal blue two-button blazer with matching slacks. "I could have told you there was no reason to go out today."

"I would have gone anyway," I muttered, picking up the controller and putting it on the couch. "You know how stubborn I am."

"I do, indeed," Larry nodded. "What time is your contact supposed to arrive?"

"Sundown at latest. Luc is pretty punctual about things. I trust him."

Larry smiled and ran his fingers through his hair distractedly. "You are the strangest Keeper I have ever met, Thomas Statford. You are brash, headstrong, stubborn."

"Thanks, I think." I gave a slight grin in return.

"You are honorable, foolish, reckless and capable of great acts of heroism." Larry stood. "Amongst your collection of friends and family are an assassin, a government agent, a medical examiner, two police officers and the head of a government agency so secretive even I cannot even think of gaining access to it. You have people who can and do follow you into the fires."

I shrugged, not sure where this was coming from. "Yeah, I am pretty lucky. What's the point?"

"Do not take them for granted, Thomas." Larry's eyes got far away, as if he were gazing into a deep abyss. "Believe me, you are fortunate to have them. One day, you could wake up and they would be gone."

"I know. They're my world." I laughed and added, "You're part of that family."

The spirit actually blushed and looked at his feet shyly. "My thanks, Thomas. You honor me."

I gave Larry a big grin and went to the kitchen to make a sandwich. Larry's little outburst of touchy-feely was quite unexpected. I had no idea what he was trying to tell me or where this mass of emotion was coming from, but I appreciated it. Even with the list of allies Larry named, I was pretty much standing on my own. What was worse, I had no backup if I had to go into a bad place. Sure, it wouldn't be the first time, but I has trying to keep that from happening anymore in my advancing age.

I chewed thoughtfully, trying to make sense of the last several days. Bad dreams, people blowing themselves up or carving major organs from their own bodies, and sheer craziness from all sides. I had very little to go on besides the universe being crazier than the gods, and the universe deciding to visit that craziness upon me. From all indications, these lunatics were just doing these things for the fun of it.

When I finished eating, I felt a bit better. Not a lot, but a bit. I sat on the couch and began playing video games again to pass the time. I called Larry over to show him the game and get scolded for engaging in such pointless exercises. That may not sound like a good time, but Larry had developed a cutting tongue over the thousands of years, and he enjoyed heaping abuse on me when I welcomed it. It helped pass the time, and it was easier than before to get lost in mindless fun.

The doorbell rang hours later, just before sunset. I had turned off the games and was catching up on my reading when the bell went off. Pulling my gun and holding it behind my back, I walked to the door and checked the peephole. Outside was a small person with a hood, their head bent down against the wind. The fisheye lens distorted the view, but gave every indication that my visitor was alone.

"Who is it?" I called out.

The voice that came back was soft, nearly lost between the speaker and the door. "I represent the Stopper of Thoughts."

No one would use Luc's professional name lightly, so I called it legitimate. I opened the door to a person five feet tall exactly. A long white cloak covered the visitor, a sheen of snow on it. The garment was closed, keeping the warmth in most likely. "Come on in."

The messenger's head shook slightly. "Regrettably, Mr. Statford, I cannot. My mentor requires my presence elsewhere."

"Okay." Can't say I didn't try to be nice. "Got a name?"

"I am Lisa Apate, Mr. Statford. My mentor wishes me to give you this address." The cloak parted and her hand held out a small slip of paper. "He wished to give it to you himself, but he is currently dealing with a situation appropriate to his station. I'm sure you understand."

After putting my gun at the small of my back, I took the small slip and smiled. "Thank you, Miss Apate. I'll be happy to let your mentor know you've done well."

The hood stayed low, but I could see the slight smile my words brought. "My thanks, Mr. Statford. I must go now." The cloak closed around her and just like Luc had the night before, she walked on top of the snow, leaving nearly no sign of her passage. I really had to learn that trick.

I closed the door and checked the paper. It was an address with which I had some familiarity: the warehouse district in downtown Newport News. Not the greatest area of town, but it had gotten better over the years. There were plenty of places a group of nuts could hide out and never be found.

"Good news, I take it?" Larry glanced at the paper and nodded. "So you are going to end this."

"Yeah. It's time." I shuddered at my choice of words. They had been an unconscious choice. I shrugged off the feeling of dread and put on my coat. "Let's get a move on."

Darkness fell like a hammer, the sun racing away from the sky. The snow finally started to taper off, though a flurry flew here and there as I drove. I made a conscious decision not to call anyone then, as this was my problem. I promised myself that if it looked like more than I could handle, I would call someone. The Toyota had a police radio, so I would have no problem getting in contact with help then. For a looksee, though? I didn't want to tip off whoever was at that address if they were listening to a police scanner.

The drive itself took an hour and a half, and I was worn out by the slips and slides and close calls with ditches. I sat in a lot near the warehouse, watching it closely with the lights and engine off. The cold advanced as the heat abated, but I wanted to catch my breath first. I likely wouldn't get a second chance at this.

The lot had no other cars, but plenty of steel transport containers. I had parked next to one of the larger ones, the bulky container obscuring me from the warehouse. The snowfall had been haphazard, leaving some spots between the containers clear of ice. With the car shut off, I could hear the wind blowing, though not as loudly as it had earlier. As with most warehouses in the district, this one was a bit run down.

"Larry, do a once-around the place real quick." I pulled my gun again and popped the magazine to check the loads. When Larry returned and gave the place a clean bill of health, I took a deep breath. "Okay, let's do it."

I pushed the door open and stepped out into the biting cold weather. My breath plumed with each exhale, burning on the inhale. I transferred my Beretta to my right coat front pocket and buttoned the coat around me. My hands went into the coat pockets past the wrist, the leather doing its best to trap my body heat and keep my fingers from freezing. The last thing I wanted was to be caught unable to pull my gun just because I was too dumb to keep my hands warm.

Deciding that a long black leather coat in a huge amount of white would not hide me one bit even with darkness falling, I took off at a fast walk to the front of the warehouse, trying to watch everywhere, checking for ambushes or even cameras. There was nothing around. The unreality washed over me again, the sense of being the only human being for miles weighed on my mind. I shook it off and made my way the couple of hundred paces to the warehouse's door. I wondered if it was locked, but a snippet from an old book I once read bubbled up to the surface of my brain.

Places like this are never locked.

The knob turned soundlessly beneath my hand, and the door swung inward without a sound. Not wanting to make myself any more a target than I already was, I slipped inside and closed the door as quietly as I could. The room I found myself in was an office, brightly lit with a desk, table lamp, and several filing cabinets. It looked like something out of Central Casting, commonplace and just like every other office that existed in movies and real life. It was normal and boring, a place to file in the brain as just another regular office.

I kicked my mind into high gear. That was when the differences hit me. The desk was spotless, with no papers anywhere in sight. Not even the filing baskets were burdened with paper of any kind. The blotter was pristine; there was not even so much as a smudge of ink on it, let alone doodles, numbers or names. On the blotter was a calendar with no notes on it. I suspected if I opened the filing cabinets, I would find row upon row of empty folders looking like they had just come out of the local office supply store. Someone went to a lot of trouble to make this look like a regular office, and it was good enough to throw off casual observers. Unfortunately for them, I am not a casual observer.

Across from the entrance was another door I assumed would lead further into the warehouse. Another oddity struck me: there were no windows anywhere in the office, not even for a foreman or manager to check on their workers. I reached into my coat pocket for my gun and pulled it out, keeping it pointed down and against my leg. Even though the place screamed "phony" to me, I didn't want to take the chance of plugging some schmuck for having an excruciatingly clean and organized office.

I gave the warehouse proper entrance knob a tentative twist, and it turned easily. With the door opened a crack, I looked through it into the warehouse itself. From my limited view, I saw a shelf reaching the ceiling, stuffed with cardboard boxes wrapped in plastic with every box wedged tightly together, allowing no light between them. Overhead lights blazed down, the bulbs glaring with a brilliance to rival the sun. I held my breath and listened carefully, trying to discover if there was anything my eyes were missing.

Nothing. It was quiet as a tomb.

Shrugging off the uncomfortable thought, I opened the door wide enough for me to slip through, my gun hand searching for possible targets. I desperately wished for eyes in the back of my head while I made my way to the shelf. Looking from one side to the other, I estimated the office was set about midway between walls, leaving me in about the center of the shelving. With my back pressed to the boxes, I made my way to the right as I was now facing, leading with my gun. When the sound of my coat against the cardboard was too loud, I separated from it by bare inches.

I moved slowly, the only sounds being my breath and an occasional loud footstep by me. Whenever I put my foot down too hard, I stopped and listened to see if I had been discovered. Of course, by that point, I was just about convinced that there was nobody there, and Luc had gotten a bad tip. It happened rarely, but it happened. When I reached the corner, I peeked around and saw another long set of shelves. It fit snugly with the set I had been hiding against, going all the way to the ceiling.

Doing the math in my head, I had gone about a hundred yards in one direction, which made the far end of the warehouse two hundred yards away. That was about when the creeps started in. I was in a huge warehouse full of goods, it was the week before Christmas, and there wasn't a single soul or a single sound in the entire place. Something in my head wanted me to turn around and haul ass, but I pushed it away, figuring it to be the scared little voice that usually screamed at me to run away from the gaping jaws of death. It wasn't until I was two-thirds down the next side of the warehouse that I recognized it as the reasonable sane voice.

And it was scared.

Figuring it to be too late to turn back, I kept going, making my way to the next corner. Another thing struck me as odd. Two sides of this shelving and I had yet to find a way into the internal area. For all intents and purposes, they were two solid walls of metal and merchandise. Most warehouses put things in columns, while this place put the boxes of stuff in just about the most inefficient way possible.

I took another look around the corner and saw more of the same, the only change a door in the middle of the wall. If I hadn't been paying attention, I would have thought I was looking at where I came in. I promised myself if I got all the way around and didn't find a way to the center of the stacks, I would get in the car and find some help. This was getting too strange, even for me. Even then, I continued on.

Just when I was almost opposite the door, I heard the knob rattle. It was no more than twenty feet away. I sprinted to the side of the door, where I was invisible to anyone who tried to look through a cracked-open door. I held my breath, the Beretta heavy in my hand as I raised it so the barrel pointed at the ceiling. With an almost imperceptible creak, the door opened.

A gloved hand holding a Glock came through that doorway, followed by a maroon and orange jacketed arm. At a guess, the owner of the arm and therefore the gun was only about five foot six. I leveled the gun at the appropriate height for the head and waited.

The head of Susana Statford filled my sights as she finished walking through the doorway. She was wearing the Virginia Tech jacket I gave her for her birthday. Her hair was pulled back, though two locks framed her face, and her cheeks were red, likely from the cold outside. When she was all the way through, she turned to her right and saw me. Susana let out a small cry before dropping her arm to her side. I let out a curse and raised the pistol again to point at the ceiling. "What the hell are you doing here?" I hissed.

"What the hell do you mean by that?" Susana held her left hand to her chest, seeming to try and catch her breath or slow her heart rate. Having a gun pointed at you can have that kind of effect. "Why were you pointing a gun at me?"

I moved away from her back toward the shelves, the better to keep an eye on anything that might come from either side of us. I beckoned her over and kept my voice low. "Because other than you, there is no one else in this warehouse."

"You do know there was a pretty bad blizzard last night and this morning, right?" Susana put her gun away. "We're probably the only people stupid or crazy enough to be here."

"Keep it down!" I put my finger to my lips. "Babe, things are just way too weird around here. Renton's in the hospital, my sister thinks I'm crazy and paranoid, and I've seen two people kill themselves right in front of me. Come on." I began moving the way I was going earlier. "Watch the back. Something is really wrong."

After fifty yards, the fact that Susana was there finally clicked. "Wait a godsdamned minute," I muttered. I came to a stop so quickly, Susana bumped into me. "What are you doing here? I sent you to your father's place."

Looking at me and smiling patiently, she nodded. "Yeah, *gringo*, until you told me it was okay to come back. I got on the jet and got back here about an hour ago."

My mouth was dry. "I didn't call you back here."

"You sent me a text saying that everything was okay, and you figured out my present for you." Susana pulled out her phone and showed it to me. She was right. Right under my name was a message saying I knew her gift, and she could come back because it was just about over.

"I haven't gotten my phone fixed, Susana."

Her tanned face paled. "You didn't send this?" I shook my head no. "Then you don't know I'm pregnant?"

My brain locked in shock. "You're what?"

"I'm pregnant. We're having a baby."

Oh fuck. Oh please gods no.

"Run," I wheezed. That was when things clicked together. Blood of the innocent. "Fuck."

"What?" Susana took her gun out again.

"Fucking run!" I grabbed her free hand with mine to head for the doorway.

We made it maybe half a dozen yards before the lights went out, leaving us in pitch blackness.

Susana's breathing was heavy as I pulled her close to me. "Back to back," I whispered. "Your hand in my pocket. Stay close."

"Tommy?" Fear was in her voice, not something I had heard in years.

"It's going to be okay, babe." I began edging for where I thought the door was. "Just stay close to me."

We walked like that for a few steps, straining to hear anything that didn't belong to us. I was breathing shallowly, trying to stay quiet. Susana bumped into me constantly, and with every contact I felt her heart hammering.

To my left and ahead, I heard the scrape of a shoe, not forty feet away. My gun swiveled towards the noise and fired. Even with the gunshot, I heard a muffled cry of pain. The muzzle flash lit the dark like a momentary sun, and my heart caught in my throat. In the brief light, I saw the forms of a dozen men, all coming toward us.

Trying to gauge their locations and correcting with each flash, I fired again and again, my bullets striking home. Behind me, I heard the bark of Susana's Glock, the punching cardboard sound hammering my ears. We fired our guns empty, and I felt her hand leave my pocket to reload. I did the same, but screamed for her to grab on to me, that we were going to get out of there.

Gods help me, though, it felt like a lie.

The slide on the Beretta clicked forward, the bullet chambered. I didn't feel Susana grab my coat, and I called to her, reaching with my empty hand. I heard a clicking noise that sounded so familiar. When I felt the metal prongs enter the flesh of my left hand, I recognized the sound.

Seventy thousand volts flashed through me, pitching me forward to the ground. I involuntarily snuffled dust in my noise as I tried breathing. I tried pushing myself up, my muscles barely responding, but trying to come back under my command. That act of defiance ended quickly as another jolt sent me into spasms on the floor. My gun fell out of my hand, clinking on the stone ground.

There were another pair of jolts from the TASER, the clicking lost in the soundless scream that I tried to make. I couldn't move, and it was getting to the point that breathing was becoming a luxury I could not afford. I felt rough hands on me, pulling my coat off. Dimly I heard my gun kicked away as I got another shot from the stun gun. I felt my shirt being ripped open and I was thrown onto my stomach. There was a savage pinch on my right bicep, and I felt the world fade away.

My last thoughts as I descended into perceptual blackness were of Susana, and how I failed her. Two words went through my head.

Wake up.

Chapter Twelve

It was a long road back to consciousness, with demons in white spitting lightning chasing me the entire way. The stone floor was cold to the touch, my bare chest and arms on it, gooseflesh rippling wherever I was exposed to the open air. My head pounded like a kettle drum, my pulse a rhythmic piledriver on my brain. I was flat on my stomach, and I could feel a trickle of blood from a wound on the right side of my head. I tried bringing my hands to my head, to ease the thumping in my skull, but whenever I tried, I couldn't do it. I risked opening my eyes a sliver, which granted piercing light access to my sensitive eyes. My eyes squeezed shut involuntarily, but I forced them open again. A wave of vertigo hit me, even though I was completely still, and I felt my stomach heave. I lifted up by reflex and vomited up everything I had eaten in what felt like the last thousand years.

Morphine, or something damned near to it, my mind reported, trying to stay objective, trying to give me something to latch on to so I could pull myself together. I spat on the floor, trying to clear my mouth without my hands. I finally noticed I was on my knees, my arms tied at the wrist, one to each side. A feeling of déjà vu washed over me, but I couldn't quite place it. My right bicep hurt like a bastard, and I remembered that was where I had been stuck when me and Susana---

"No!" I screamed, or at least tried to scream. It came out as more a croak than anything forceful. I looked around, trying to get an idea of where I was.

It was an open area, lit from nine iron braziers. The flames were well-tended, shedding light and heat, though I actually felt very little of the latter. I got the feeling we were still inside, but not what we were inside. The light didn't extend far enough to where the walls were, and the floor was non-descript solid stone. Attached to each wrist, spreading my arms wide, was a leather strap, secured to an eyebolt set into the floor. An experimental tug proved I was stuck, and I couldn't get the leverage to pull free. Underneath me was a design of some kind, like something out of an old movie set, or from those Ancient Aliens shows, where extraterrestrials gave the secrets of carving stone or something to a bunch of primitives.

I raised my head and looked directly ahead of me. There was an altar, carved of granite, glyphs and stylized pictures of birds all over it. It was old, so godsdamned old, I could feel the age coming off it, pulsing in time to my head. There were ruddy stains all over the sides, and I knew without a doubt it was blood. I had seen old dried blood before; it wasn't a sight I would forget easily. A coppery tang was on the air, invading my senses and getting the reptilian part of my brain, the one that screamed fight or flight, the one that registered raw pure fear, yammering at me to get loose, to get free, to run until my legs fell off, then pull myself even farther until my hands were bloody and useless.

When my eyes got to the top of the altar, I stopped breathing. All the wind went from my lungs, my mouth went dry, my heart stopped beating.

There lay Susana, wearing some kind of bright white robe of thin cloth. Her eyes were closed, her chest rising and falling very slowly. Her arms were innocent of clothing, the skin showing signs of the cold. I could see her hands were laying on her stomach, the fingers interlaced. Her hair was fanned out underneath her, her head lying on a stone. There were a pair of wide leather straps across her left arm, and I guessed her right as well, securing her to the altar.

Gods, I had seen this movie before. I knew how it went.

I managed to get to my feet and began pulling on the right strap securing me to the floor. The leather cut into my wrist, blood seeping from the abrasions. I strained as hard as I could, which wasn't that much. I was still weak from the morphine shot, and as bad as my head hurt, it was likely I had multiple doses still running through me. The pain was secondary, almost non-existent in my mind. I had to get free. I had to save Susana.

I had to save her and our child.

After pulling for I have no idea how long, I dropped to my knees and wept. All I had succeeded in doing was rubbing my right wrist nearly to the bone. The blood, my blood, didn't even work as a lubricant to help me slip out; the bonds were too tight. I found my voice and let loose a scream of frustration at the roof, wherever it was. No words, just an inarticulate howl of anguish.

As I knelt in the circle, I heard a voice behind me. "It is well you are with us of your own accord, Keeper." It was an old, no, ancient voice that had not the weight of years, but centuries. It was a mild voice, one that conjured images of the wise man at the top of the mountain, or the shamans of the plains. There was no anger there, no cruelty. There was only a sadness, like when performing a chore you hate to do, but it had to be done anyway.

I craned my head around in the direction the words came from and saw him. If he was less than eighty, I would eat the candles off his last birthday cake, lit and all. There was still power in his movement as he circled around me, giving me a wide berth. I couldn't have grabbed him anyway, as he was just out of reach. I noted the caution in his steps, though; it was born of fear and respect of me. The green feathered headdress fit him perfectly, framing his weathered skin, his high cheekbones, his square jaw. A beak of gold stuck out from the headdress. His robe was also covered in green, with yellow and red feathers adding to the construction of it. Where most would feel self-conscious and ridiculous, he looked regal, as if born to wear such a costume.

"What the fuck is going on here?" I was shouting, trying to use whatever I could for advantage. What I had was not much.

The old man shook his head sadly. "I think you know, Keeper."

"Bullshit! You want me, fine. Leave her out of this!" I pulled again on my bonds, the leather creaking but holding.

"That is not for me to say. I am only a tool of the gods." He clapped his hands once, sharply, and the old man façade was gone. That one clap seemed to energize him, give him the power to rejuvenate himself, even if only in spirit. "It is very well, Keeper."

From the darkness surrounding us, I saw at least a dozen other men clad in a lesser version of the high priest's outfit. Wristbands of feathers, coverings of feathers and leather laces on their calves, loincloths. I felt out of time, as if we had somehow gone to some long ago century where the Spanish weren't even aware of the legends of streets paved with gold.

"Look, just let her go," I begged. I was babbling, and I was flat-out begging. "Don't do this to her, please! She has nothing to do with it!"

The high priest walked behind the altar, his steps slow and measured. He looked at a cheap digital watch on his wrist, a complete anachronism that utterly flummoxed me. "We have time, Keeper. Time enough to talk."

"Then just release her, man! She's not part of this!" Tears were hot in my throat.

Wearily, the priest shook his head again. "There's where you're wrong. She has a big part to play in this, as do we." He lifted his hand and pointed at me, the wrinkled and dry digit firm and unwavering. "As do you." He lowered his hand again, supporting himself on the altar. "We all have things we must do, whether we want to do them or not. One of your people once said that all the world is a stage, and we are just players. He was right."

"What the fuck are you talking about?" I was completely confused and within about a tenth of a second from panicking. "You think Shakespeare told you to do this?"

He laughed at that. Not much, but noticeable. "No, Keeper. You do not understand. One of the prophets of the gods asked about the potter and the potter's clay. We are but tools of the potter."

I spat on the ground, red mixed in with the spittle. "I take back what I thought of you. I thought you weren't completely crazy. Turns out you're nuttier than squirrel shit."

"We are not, Keeper. We are merely tools, like your gun, or your phone, or your car." He took a breath and indicated the dozen or so men who surrounded us. Two pairs approached me, one pair for each side. "We hold no rancor for you, even though you killed several of our brothers, because we are nothing more than living tools."

My mind raced, trying to play for time. "So that's why those two killed themselves? They thought they were a defective hammer or something? Are you serious?" I twisted my wrists clockwise and back, trying to get free. "You didn't want to kill me. I know that much. What I don't know is why."

The high priest pursed his lips in thought. "Do you know what today is, Keeper?"

"You knocked me out, asshole. It could be fucking Arbor Day for all I know." I felt two pairs of strong hands grip my shoulders and arms.

The old man said something in that clipped language, and the hands loosened. "Please forgive my sons. They are anxious for us to be about our business. This is the culmination of thousands of years, and they are impatient."

I shrugged off the grip and actually tried biting one of the bastards. "Tell you what: let her go and we'll call it even."

"Her part is not yet done in this." The priest nodded his head. "Today is December 20th, Keeper, and we are only a few minutes from midnight."

"What the hell are you talking about?" The date clicked in my head. "Oh shit, you mean that stupid conspiracy theory? The end of the world? The Mayan Doomsday from a couple of years ago?" I started laughing. It was a low chuckle at first, then a booming laughter that came from my gut. Tears streamed down my eyes as I tried to stop. "You think the world's going to end because of a prophecy that didn't fucking happen!" I sobered quickly, snarling at the old priest. "The deadline was years ago! It was a hoax! A thousand-year-old bunch of bullshit!"

"No, Keeper. It is real." One of the other men brought forth an oblong gold box and placed it in the priest's outstretched hand. With practiced ease, he opened it with one hand and removed a glittering black knife. The thing looked sharp enough to cut anything. "We changed the date because you were not ready."

The hands gripped me again and I pulled away. "What are you talking about?" Confusion struck me again as I thought back to the year the Mayans said the world would end. What did he mean ready? There was nothing different between then and now.

That was when it hit me. There was one thing different. Susana and I weren't together.

The priest smiled sadly. "Now you understand. Now you see."

Hands gripped me solidly. "You sons of bitches. You don't know how fucked you are."

"Really, Keeper?" The priest tilted his head at me. "How so?"

"The master of assassins knows where I went. He sent me there. When he doesn't hear from me, he'll come looking." I tried twisting out of the way but to no avail. "I know what he can do. You let her go now, you get to live."

"Oh. That." The old priest shrugged. "He does not know where you are. That was not his apprentice you met."

My mouth dropped open. Oh gods, no.

"We took great pains to take away anyone who could help you. The assassin. The agent. The police. The mother. The sister." The old man ticked off each point on a finger, the tip of the blade touching the fingertips. "We did this not because we wanted to, but because we were commanded to do so."

"Who, you mealy-mouthed son of a bitch?" I tried pulling away and could not.

"Please know that we do not do this out of spite," the priest said, his tone pleading. "Had we our way, we would not do this. However, we must all perform our parts. Your role is not over, Keeper, though you may wish it. I am sorry, but this is the end."

I pulled toward the altar as hard as I could, feeling my shoulders creak and pull in their sockets. My captors lost their grip on me for a moment. "I will fucking gut you all!" I screamed, a spray coming from my mouth. "You touch her, I swear by all the gods there have ever been, are and shall be, I will kill you. I will strip the godsdamned skin from your fucking bones and I will enjoy every motherfucking second of it!"

With a voice of unending sadness, the priest shook his head a final time. "No, Keeper, you will not." He nodded his head once to the ones holding me. "Our orders are clear, my sons. Make him watch."

It was at that moment Susana's eyes opened. She lifted her head and tried to sit up, but was kept in place by the leather bands. I heard her voice faintly saying my name.

"Tommy? Where are you?"

"I will end you fuckers!" I raved. I screamed. I felt hands in my hair and against my head, keeping me facing the altar. "Leave her alone!"

"Tommy, what's going on?" Oh gods, she was becoming aware. "What happened?"

The priest raised his arms in supplication, to who or what I had no idea, and I didn't care. I watched the glittering obsidian knife in his hand weave delicate patterns above my wife. Words of antiquity sounding from his lips, echoing off of something and building up power.

"Larry!" I screamed in desperation.

"I am here, Thomas," came the words of my oldest and dearest friend. "Oh gods, no."

"Do something! Stop them!" I pleaded. I had no idea what a disembodied spirit could do, but there had to be some trick he could pull off.

"Here, now!" Larrisimus bellowed with the force of a battering ram. "Release that woman!"

I don't know what I expected. I didn't think they would even take notice of a spirit only I could see, and who couldn't physically interact with anything in the world. It was desperation, plain and simple. It was all I had left.

Larry stepped into my field of view, his clothing changed into that armor I had seen before. It shimmered in the light, pearlescent and beautiful. A sword of pure light was in his hand, and he pointed it at the high priest. "In the name of the Conclave and all the gods that are, were or shall be, I command you to cease this at once!"

Even I stopped struggling for a brief second. I felt hope spring in my chest, blooming in an instant and filling me with the possibility that things just might work out. I started pulling at my bonds harder, fueled by the light of Larrisimus. For that moment, I thought it would work.

How utterly foolish.

The priest paused in his chant and fixed Larry with a baleful eye. As Larry advanced on him, the old man spoke, clearly and succinctly. "Sprit, know thy Self."

The sword vanished in an instant, as did the armor. Larry stumbled to his knees, clad only in a tunic and breeches. He reared back, kneeling on his heels, and howled in utter agony. I could only make out a few words, the ones used most being that he remembered. He pulled at his hair, screaming again and again that he remembered everything, that he was sorry, that he did not know what was happening, that he remembered it all now.

As Larry rolled into a fetal ball, somewhere, a lone bell began to chime, and the priest muttered two final words.

"It's time."

"Tommy!" Susana screamed, and the knife fell.

There was a roar in my ears as I screamed my wife's name, as I watched the first cut, as I saw the first jet of blood geyser up from the wound. The second bell brought another cut, and the sound of ribs breaking. I screamed again, my throat nearly breaking from the strain. Each of the next eight bells brought further desecration and destruction to Susana. Bright crimson flew all over the priest, the liquid painting him in gore. Some got on the beak of his headdress, making it look like the bird had a part in the murder as her blood, my beautiful Susana's blood dripped back down into the hole that monster was making in her chest.

I screamed again. All I could do was scream until I thought my voice would rip my throat to shreds. I struggled more, but in vain. The arms weren't even holding me anymore. I couldn't turn away if I tried. Her head turned towards me, and I watched her mouth trickling blood, my beautiful Susana trying to live just one more minute, one more second, and I saw her eyes. They locked onto mine, and even then, when she knew there was no way I could save her, no way to keep this horror from happening to her, I still saw her hope and her love for me.

Oh gods. Why did you all allow this? Why did I allow this?

The eleventh chime, and the priest performed a quick circle around her heart. On the final sounding, the one that officially made the date December 21st, he lifted the heart of Susana Magdalena Statford to the heavens, with one last plea in whatever language he used. I couldn't hear it.

I was watching the light go out in her eyes.

Tears poured down my face, burning hot. Blood flowed from her heart down his upraised arm, the lines a red tattoo of death. I pulled my bonds, not caring if my hands were cut off at the wrist, just pulling and yanking and growling and calling out her name. I watched my world ending right before me, and there was nothing I could do about it.

With what could only be the last of her strength and her life, she mouthed three words to me, her lips crimson. There was a peaceful smile on her face as she formed them, a counterpoint to the horrors that were visited upon her. I mouthed them back, knowing she couldn't hear them.

Then, her eyes glossed, she constricted and then instantly slack.

She was gone.

I leaned forward, my forehead touching the stone floor. I wasn't even making any more noise, my throat was so destroyed. There was nothing left to me. My eyes refused to open as I wept silently.

"It is done, Keeper."

My muscles thrummed as I renewed my assault on the leather holding me back. I wasn't thinking of anything but ripping their throats out with my teeth if necessary. All I wanted was their blood on my hands. I needed it, hungered for it, desired it. I was little more than an animal wanting to play with their flesh and bones and sinew. I would have my vengeance.

"She is playing her part in this, as did we." The priest walked to the foot of the altar. Her life painted a macabre tableau on his face and robe. "Your part is not yet over, though." I snapped at him like a dog. "All things come to an end, Keeper, good or bad." I watched all but two assemble in front of me, between me and the altar. One stayed to each side of me, and they all pulled out their own stone knives. "This is the end."

The priest took the obsidian knife and brought it to the middle-left of his chest, the others mirroring him with their own blades. As one, they thrust the knives into their hearts. None of them made a sound, not even a grunt of discomfort. They dropped to their knees, then to their sides. The two to the sides of me pulled their knives from their chests, showering me with hot red blood, and cut my bonds. I stumbled forward and fell into a pair of bodies. The warm jets of the red stuff were slowing as they bled out, but I felt the fluids on me.

I pushed myself off them and pulled myself up the altar. I gagged at the sight of what had been done to her, my throat constricting, my stomach reeling. I brought myself to face her, the softness in her features, the lack of breath, the emptiness of her eyes all telling me what my heart and soul refused to believe.

I whispered my love to her, my unending, undying love, and I kissed her, tasting her life on my lips. I held her head close to me, trying to be gentle. She was already growing cold, already gone from me forever.

Looking around me, I saw that the bastards had taken away even revenge from me. I had lost everything. I had nothing. I had nothing left.

My voice came from my mouth and cursed the gods. I cursed them until I was repeating myself, and I got louder, shouting at them, gripping the body of my wife and mother of my unborn child close to me. With every word, my voice climbed, higher and higher. I don't even know what I said, and I didn't care; I wanted the heavens to fall.

With a final scream, I flung my right hand, wet with both her blood and my own, at the sky. I shouted one final curse at those I blamed for this atrocity.

"Let the heavens fall!"

And everything went white.

Epilogue

"He's coming around, Doctor."

My first thought was I was blind. I thought that because it was dark. Pitch dark. There was nothing around me but blackness, an abyss I felt I belonged in. The smell of antiseptic and burning hair assaulted my nose. I tried moving my hands to my eyes, but something stopped them. I pulled again, but not too hard; something said it was okay, that I should relax.

No, not okay. This wasn't okay at all. This was a bad place. They knew who and what I was. They wanted to hurt me. Best to just play along, make them think I'm going along with it.

Going along with what, I asked myself in the dark.

It, you idiot. Go along with it.

"Hello?" A kind and gentle voice broke through the bickering in my head. "Are you still with us?"

I tried to answer, but there was something in my mouth. My tongue touched it and instantly retreated as far as it could. The taste of the rubber was foul, just as the air I pulled through the hole in the mouthpiece was rank. It was the taste of desperation and despondency, and I felt as if I was just taking more and more of it in with every breath.

"No need to talk yet." That was the first voice. It was a helpful voice, one used to taking commands and helping others. I knew this voice. I knew it well, but from where? "We need to get you back to your room."

"The coverings first, Andre." The second voice was so cultured, so in control. It was a voice of command, and though usually gentle, it could whipsnap into harshness at the drop of a hat. "I believe he would like to see where he's going."

"Of course, Doctor." It was then I realized I hadn't been able to move my head at all. I was completely immobilized. I felt a release of pressure that I didn't know was there, and I could move. Not much, but enough that a sigh of relief escaped me.

"You see, Andre? He's just fine. Now, the eye coverings first, please."

Two things rang through my mind when I felt the cold steel against my cheek and I heard the snipping of scissors. One, I didn't know where I was. I didn't know who was cutting whatever was covering my eyes off my head. I didn't know what was going on.

The second thing was that I knew who these two men were. I knew what they were doing. I knew why I had my eyes covered; it was for my own safety since I blacked out sometimes during sessions.

Light burned my eyes as the gauze circles came off. I squinted in reflex, trying to see where I was.

A face, smooth and young, leaned over me and flashed a penlight into my eyes. "You gave us quite the scare!" Though chiding me, there was a friendly smile on his face. "How are you feeling?"

The second voice, Andre, reached over with a huge hand and pulled the mouthpiece free. "Now he can answer you, Doctor Odentson." Andre sounded pleased for himself. He busied himself with my wrists, removing the restraints.

My first words were not what I wanted, nor what I expected. "Who the fuck are you? Where the hell am I?"

The doctor looked a bit crestfallen. "Oh, dear. We're back to that again? I thought we were past these episodes. You must have missed some of your medication. You're thinking you're your alter-ego again. We can't have that."

"I'm sorry," I said, and I really was. "I don't know what came over me, Doctor."

A tight smile crossed his face. "It's all right. I have just the thing." From the pocket of his white coat, he pulled out a syringe. Pulling off the plastic covering, he checked the dosage.

Arm's free, my mind reported. Now or never.

Like a viper, I slipped my hands from the restraints and grabbed the doctor by his lapels. "Where the fuck am I?" I gave him a shake and pulled his face to mine. "Who are you? What are you doing to me? Who am I? What is going on? Why am I here?"

"Andre, restrain him!" The doctor kept the syringe out and free as massive hands closed over my wrists and squeezed. I let out a gasp of pain and released the doctor's coat. Like a rag doll, my arms were held above my head.

"Come on, you weren't supposed to do that!" Andre's face was scant inches from mine, and his breath was atrocious. My head automatically tried to butt his, but he pulled back easily. "Now, now. That's not very nice."

"Do you have him, Andre?" When Andre answered yes, Doctor Odentson plunged the needle into my arm.

Blessed relief flowed through my body and I just went limp. My head went fuzzy, and I didn't want to fight anymore. I looked over to the doctor and smiled.

"I'm sorry, Doctor Odentson, I really am."

"It's okay," he said, somewhat out of breath. "I thought we were making progress."

I nodded sleepily. Sounds were starting to echo, and I was seeing trails. It was altogether relaxing.

"Andre is going to take you to your room."

"That's right," Andre said, easily depositing me in a wheelchair. He had to be nearly seven feet tall, though in my state, he might as well have been a thousand. I giggled at his hair, and how red it was. "It's going to be okay. I'll get you right where you need to go."

"Doc?" I slurred.

"Yes?"

"Can I ask you a favor?" Man, it was hard to keep my head up and my eyes open.

"If I can, I will."

"Can you tell me who I am?"

And thus ends Volume V of the Statford Chronicles. Be ready for Volume VI: A Tangled Web, and as always, thank you for your support.

www.ingramcontent.com/pod-product-compliance
Lightning Source LLC
Chambersburg PA
CBHW071237130626

46556CB00003B/1056